To Sing a New Song

A Breakthrough to a New Life

BY
LOUANN STAHL

eShore

Pittsburgh, PA

2002

ISBN 1-58501-034-0

Trade Paperback
© Copyright 2002 Louann Stahl
All Rights Reserved
First Printing — 2002
Library of Congress #2001094626

Request for information should be addressed to:

CeShore
SterlingHouse Publisher, Inc.
The Sterling Building
440 Friday Road
Pittsburgh, PA 15209
www.sterlinghousepublisher.com

CeShore is an imprint of SterlingHouse Publisher, Inc.
Cover Design: Michelle S. Lenkner — SterlingHouse Publisher, Inc.
Book Design: Kathleen M. Gall

Printed in the United States of America

"Sing Unto the Lord a New Song"

Isaiah 43:10

With faith in the future
this book is lovingly dedicated
to my grandchildren:
Anna, Daphne, Max and Jack,
and to all children everywhere.

TABLE OF CONTENTS

FOREWORD

John White, MAT
Author of *The Meeting of Science and Spirit* and
What Is Enlightenment?

If you've ever wondered what life is all about …
If you've ever asked yourself whether God exists …
If you've ever struggled with philosophical questions and
    metaphysical issues …
If you've ever been struck still by the beauty of a flower or a
    lake or a sunset …
If you've ever pondered the relationship between yourself and
    society …
If you've ever worked for social change in hopes of building a
    better world …

this book will speak deeply to you.

The author, Louann Stahl, deals wisely with these topics
and many others related to them, such as modern science,
the economics of peace and plenty, and where we're going on
Planet Earth. She does so in a style which is clear and
engaging, with a logical flow, convincing data, relevant examples and a growing sense of revelation which will speak to
you, the reader, personally, at the core of your being.

The platform from which she launches her presentation

is known as the Perennial Philosophy. It is also called the Timeless Wisdom. Stahl describes it as "the emerging paradigm." Paradoxically, this emergent worldview is very ancient.

In simplest form, the Perennial Philosophy or Timeless Wisdom is the collective highest wisdom of humanity. It is the spiritual data base of human insight and understanding about ultimate matters such as those above. It has been accumulated from cultures around the world, from East and West, from seers and sages, from sacred paths and religious traditions, and from every endeavor by questing human beings to answer questions which are fundamental to human happiness.

The wonderful thing about the Perennial Philosophy is this: It shows that, despite differences in the name and form of those paths and traditions, there is a transcendent unity to them. They agree on fundamentals. They distill insight and understanding gained by questing human beings throughout history into a few simple propositions from which the great variations in doctrine, ritual and so forth blossom into the rich field of higher human development and cultural evolution. It shows that behind the differences apparently dividing people of various faiths and cultures, there is purpose, meaning and direction to life. There is a beautiful purpose, a hopeful meaning, an exciting direction which promises a fulfillment of outward peace and harmony through inward unification and resolution.

The name "perennial philosophy" comes from philosophia perennis, a term coined by the 17th century German philosopher Leibniz. The Perennial Philosophy is also the title of a book Aldous Huxley published in 1944 about this global wisdom-tradition. It was the first book on the topic to get wide public notice, and deservedly so because it is a magnificent work about the human condition and our potential to change it for the better.

Think of 1944. The entire world was at war. Tens of

millions of lives, military and civilian, had been lost due to the direct and indirect effects of the fighting. As the destruction and death toll increased, humanity's hopes and dreams for a peaceful world seemed to be mere fantasies.

In the midst of that nightmare, Huxley wrote The Perennial Philosophy to offer a solution to the problem of man's inhumanity to man. To put it simply, he said there will never be a better world until there are better people in it, and the place to begin building better people is with ourselves, through spiritual practices which bring our lives more and more into awareness of the unity of the human family under the fatherhood of God.

Yet the world's religions, from which most spiritual practices are derived, seemed as divided from one another as the world's nations. Their potential as a force for universal good will and spiritual brotherhood was unrealized. Earth's political bodies and religious bodies alike were in deep division and struggle. What might end the warfare and unite the human race, Huxley wondered.

The only solution, he said, lay in seeing the essential unity of the world's major religions and sacred traditions. What was that unseen unity? In a single word: enlightenment. Enlightenment, he said, is the core truth of the world's major religions and sacred traditions, no matter of what era, no matter from what civilization or culture. It is the "highest common factor"—not the lowest—among the world's spiritual traditions, religions and sacred lifeways. The Perennial Philosophy was intended to show the universality of that core truth behind the multitude of names and forms which the religious impulse—humanity's search for God—has taken throughout history.

The highest common factor—enlightenment—means knowing God directly, experientially. Huxley stated it thus: "The Perennial Philosophy is primarily concerned with the One Divine Reality substantial to the manifold world of things and lives and minds."

There are three aspects to this timeless collective wisdom, Huxley explained. First is a metaphysic, namely, the fundamental idea that Reality—with a capital R—is a divine substance; all things, he said, including lives and minds, are forms of that divine Reality, traditionally called God. Second is a psychology which says that the soul of each individual is identical with divine Reality; in other words, the ultimate identity of everyone is that divine Reality, traditionally called God. Third is an ethic which says that Man's final end—that is, the goal toward which all human life is striving—is vital awareness and understanding of that divine Reality, of the immanent and transcendent Ground of all being, tradition-ally called God.

To put it more simply, God or divine Reality is the source of all creation and we human beings are one with the source at the soul-level of our being. The purpose of human life is to consciously realize that divine source within us and then align our lives to express it throughout all our activities. We must let the Ground of our being become the basis of our doing.

That is God-realization. That is enlightenment. That is the core truth of the world's major religions and sacred tradi-tions. That is the final solution to the problem of man's perennial inhumanity to man—a spiritual solution. Huxley's research demonstrated that convincingly in his book and it has been confirmed many times over since then by scholars and spiritual teachers alike around the world.

The Perennial Philosophy has been challenged in modern times by science. The scientific tradition, while advancing us in mastery of the outer world, has undermined the inner world. It has projected a world view of existence as purely physical: random, purposeless, materialistic and godless. That world view pictures humanity as alone in a hostile universe without any purpose or significance.

The result has been the modern dilemma of material gain and spiritual loss. If there is no God, if there is no moral framework to life, if there are no ultimate values under-girding human existence and no purpose to our being-in-the-universe, then anything goes. It's dog eat dog, it's law of the jungle, it's might makes right, it's unbridled hedonism, it's violence and vulgarity, it's a race to the top of the power game, no matter by what means, and a race to the bottom of the disintegrating culture, no matter who gets hurt.

The Perennial Philosophy, Louann Stahl shows, is the way out of the dilemma. It doesn't jettison science and all its genuine gains in understanding and application. Rather, it places science in a context which transforms its results—or at least shows the way to that transformation. The world can move from a culture guided by a philosophy of godless mate-rialism to a culture based on love and wisdom which restrains, even extinguishes, the sad and painful misdirec-tions and excesses of godless materialism.

In a nutshell, then: Only the perennial philosophy can eliminate the perennial inhumanity. That is the "new song" which Louann Stahl would have us sing, and her book is a convincing demonstration of the truth to that new song. That is the "emerging paradigm" which offers the potential for a profound transformation of human consciousness and human culture. I am pleased to have this opportunity to offer readers a foreword. May her vision for "heaven on earth" be realized!

PREFACE

There has been much speculation in recent years about the 'emerging paradigm,' the new physics and chaos theory, mysticism and personal and global transformation, as well as the *big* questions, such as who we are and why we are here. In *To Sing a New Song*, these questions are addressed as interrelated phenomena leading to the re-emergence of the ancient perennial philosophy, buttressed now by the new knowledge that we have gained in science and psychology.

By examining the recent paradigms that have guided humanity's thoughts and actions, *To Sing a New Song* seeks to know what perceptions of reality have led the world into chaos and confusion, what models of behavior have been derived from these perceptions? Since we now know that order is inherent in chaos, this book explores how we may manifest it to bring about joyful, productive, abundant lives? To the question of whether there is a way to live that guarantees all people a chance for such a life and the planet a chance to heal, *To Sing a New Song* answers that there is.

To support the above thesis, this book explores the paradigm shift currently taking place due to a changing perception of the nature of reality. Led by the findings of quantum physics, chaos theory and a renewed interest in metaphysics, a change in consciousness is taking place throughout society: in the field of medicine, in the workplace, in economics, in our personal relationships, in our religious and spiritual lives.

The premise of *To Sing a New Song* indicates that this shift of perception will reveal anew that no one need have less, that someone else might have more; that harmony can replace violence in our personal and social lives; that God's Kingdom can come on earth. It would have been a cruel joke indeed—and a pointless one—if Jesus had asked us to pray for something that could not be accomplished.

The way to achieve this fulfillment has been taught to us by many sages and saints throughout history, the same wisdom that is being shared by many teachers on the scene today. *To Sing a New Song* is a synthesis of important works that includes the ancient wisdom of the perennial philosophy as well as the ideas of many writers who have brought this wisdom together with a body of modern thought. When seen together these united elements will give insight and direction as we ask the questions, who are we, why are we here, where are we going, and how are we going to get there.

As biblical wisdom has taught us, we cannot serve two masters; we must choose the belief system under which we will function. The happy news is that if enough of us (a critical mass) choose joy, love, peace and abundance for ourselves and for *all* people, we will have moved into a spiritual consciousness so strong that we must indeed bring The Kingdom forth upon the earth. With that as our aspiration we incite an ancient Vedic mantra or prayer: *= 4 chapters*

MAY WE BE LED FROM DARKNESS TO LIGHT
FROM THE UNREAL TO THE REAL
FROM DEATH TO IMMORTALITY
FROM CHAOS TO BEAUTY

SECTION I:
FROM DARKNESS TO LIGHT

"The greatest danger invariably arises from the ruthless application, on a vast scale, of partial knowledge."

E. F. Schumacher

It has been said that a little knowledge is a dangerous thing. Partial directions rarely get us to our destination. We all know that without an accurate map a traveler can become very lost. So may the traveler through life. However, we have also been assured that "ye shall know the truth, and the truth shall make you free," (John:8:32). This suggests that if we truly understand the reality of ourselves, who we are, the reality of the world in which we live, where we are, and understand why we are here, we will be free to live unencumbered by false beliefs and their consequences, as these beliefs direct our actions.

We are all born into a set of myths, beliefs, and assumptions regarding the world and our place in it. This inherited "world view" is the result of the mixture of learned experience of past generations, the state of scientific knowledge at a particular time, as well as religious and philosophical teaching. These are all interpreted through the fears, hopes and desires of the individual ego, within a social and economic context. Only when we are able to shed the chrysalis of partial truths, will we be able to emerge into the light of reality.

There is exciting evidence that this is happening. The world views of the recent past which have guided our understanding of the nature of physical reality are being profoundly challenged by new knowledge gained from quantum physics and chaos theory. There is also a growing recognition of the commonalities of the teachings of the great religious traditions. Additionally, psychology, the study of human nature, is giving us a new understanding of what it means to be human.

CHAPTER ONE

THE PREVAILING WORLD VIEWS

"Beliefs concerning the ultimate purpose and meaning of life and the accompanying worldview perspective … are critically dependent on concepts regarding the life goals and cosmic views which these allow."

Charles Leadbeater (note96)

The admonition "Know Thyself" is often quoted as the most profound teaching of Socrates. His words have echoed down the centuries. The concern of who we are and why we are here has been central to all philosophic and religious systems of thought, from the most ancient civilizations to the present day. In fact, how we answer those questions, both individually and within the communities and institutions within which we function, largely determines our way of life, our religious beliefs, and our world view.

In the western world* there are at least four major identifiable "views of man" prevalent. These four concepts of the nature of humanity either tacitly or explicitly answer the questions of who are we and why are we here.

In one view, humankind is seen as an accident of the universe. The "Big Bang" (the currently accepted cosmogony) set the universe in motion, and life has been the result of the chemical and biological interaction of matter and energy. Once life was "produced" or "evolved," the struggle and/or competition to live and endure fostered by the natural selection of chance mutations promoted the survival of the fittest individuals within a species and the survival of particular species. Thus, after billions of years, Homo-sapiens appeared, alone in an indifferent universe, to make their way as best they could.

In this view we are an accident of nature and have no purpose other than any we can devise for ourselves. Our lives and the world can be what we choose to make them, within the confines and vagaries of the given universe.

Mathew Arnold's poem, "Dover Beach," offers a stunning description of the effects of this world concept on human consciousness. In the poem's final stanza, Arnold suggests that the world

> Hath really neither joy, nor love, nor light,
> Nor certitude, nor peace, nor help for pain;
> And we are there as on a darkling plain
> Swept with confused alarms of struggle and flight,
> Where ignorant armies clash by night.

• • •

(2) The second, or "mechanistic," view of the universe also incorporates the scientific cosmogony and evolutionary theory. However, in this case, the world is seen as a Grand Machine set in motion by a Divine Intelligence with an ultimate plan. This perfect plan would work itself out through evolution, while the Grand Designer absented him/herself from the fray. Humankind, the leading edge of evolution, with the earth and its fruits as raw materials, and with the tool of science—the product of developing intelligence—would ultimately conquer nature, solve all problems and lead the way to a final utopia, the apex of human destiny.

This outlook naturally leads to a reductionist view of the world, since a machine lends itself to be taken apart, studied, and reassembled. We are then, in this scenario, hostages to destiny, cogs in a machine, working toward a preconceived Divine Plan that we as individuals cannot really know.

· · ·

Although the details of fundamentalism vary from religion to religion and even from sect to sect within a religion, this view is characterized by strict adherence to a theology set forth in a scripture said to be the exact word of God. This is believed by the adherents of the religion to be the one and only truth and the one and only path to follow to receive God's beneficence and to avoid his punishment. In this view, we are the children of an anthropomorphic Father at once compassionate, judgmental and vengeful. We are here to prove ourselves worthy, or unworthy as the case may be, to live with God in a hereafter, and to receive his promised blessings.

There are, of course, many variations of belief. Many people who adhere to a particular religion do not accept all of the fundamentalist interpretations. There are those who no longer see a vengeful God, and religion is equated more with love and compassion.

· · ·

Many people in the modern western world, Christians, Jews, Humanists, agnostics and others, are moving toward a fourth world view which I will call throughout this book "the emerging paradigm." It is, in many ways, of ancient, often eastern, origin, and has its roots in what is called in metaphysics the "perennial philosophy." The product of mystical or enlightened "knowing," the perennial philosophy has throughout the centuries been the fertile soil of the highest expression of all religions. Now that it is buttressed and enlarged by the findings of the new physics, quantum mechanics, the very new chaos theory, and new theories in psychology, it is my conviction that it is coming into full flowering in human consciousness.

The perennial philosophy recognizes the truth in all religions. This world view also incorporates the "Big Bang" cosmogony and a modified evolution theory. With new revelations about the nature of reality in physics, many philosophers of science now acknowledge some sort of self-transcendent drive in evolution. Ken Wilber, in his book *Sex, Ecology, Spirituality: The Spirit of Evolution*, suggests a more modern view of evolution limiting the role of natural selection, which "allowed science to deny any sort of eros or transcendent/emergent drive in nature." While natural selection can account for microevolution, Wilber believes the great evolutionary leaps and breakthroughs suggest some sort of self-transcendent drive operative in macroevolution.[1] The physicist Amit Goswami agrees. In an article in *The Quest*, March-April 2001, he remarks that "The gap in the fossil record suggests to quite a few biologists that Darwinism is not the complete story of evolution." He feels the fossil gap may be interpreted as "the signature of creative conscious intervention—so purpose enters evolution creatively."[2]

For most who advocate the perennial philosophy, the following generally describes their belief system. Creation is viewed as the Idea of God, A Supreme and Loving Intelligence, the animating force of the universe, both transcendent and imminent, ever present in both the macrocosm and the microcosm. All creation lives and moves and has its being within God. In fact, all individual manifestations of Creation are part of one reality, as waves are part of the ocean. Divine Love/Intelligence is the animating or vital force, the God Self, within each individual and within the universe. We are created in the image and likeness of God. Each individual has the capacity to know God, and inasmuch as we are able to realize the truth of our reality and to evolve from humanhood to our potential Christhood, or Higher Self, we are able to manifest "the kingdom of heaven" on earth.

According to Barbara Marx Hubbard in her book *The Revelation: Our Crisis is a Birth*, The Christ, in the sense that Paul spoke of "the Christ within the hope of glory," is a prepatterned potential in every human being, as the evolutionary process of the planet is prepatterned toward its rebirth in Christ consciousness. However, the existence of free will implies that while the result is probable, it is not inevitable.

The proponents of this fourth world view believe that all creation is in some way immortal—there is no death to any kind of life. Many, though not all, of those who align themselves with this metaphysical perspective believe in reincarnation, along with the evolution of the human spirit toward God Realization.

Mystical revelations through the centuries have revealed a basic picture of the nature of reality, which this emerging world view incorporates. In essence, all of God's creation is good; all things work together for the good. Although the separate ego is unreal and temporal, a construct that the separated self has made to deal with the world as we experience it, the true, God-created Self is real and eternal.

To the extent that we are attuned to and living from our divine center, we are in "heaven," which is everywhere because God is manifest everywhere. To the extent that we are living in accordance with the dictates and fears of the separate ego, we are in "hell," because hell is the sense of separation from God. Good is the essence of divine creation; evil and error are the products of the isolated ego. Therefore, those who ask why God allows evil and sin, are asking the wrong question. As Pogo said, "I've found the enemy and he is us." Through our sense of separation from each other and from God, humankind creates its own hell, as we project our limited, wrongly conceived and fearful thoughtforms upon the world.

The perennial philosophy reveres all great teachers: Krishna, Buddha, Moses, Laotse, Confucius, Muhammad, Baha'u'llah, and of course, Jesus, among many other great but lesser lights. Jesus, "the Christ" or "anointed one," is seen as the Wayshower, the One perfectly able to manifest his Divine Selfhood to demonstrate to us that we can do likewise.

In this paradigm we are no less than the manifestation of a loving Supreme Intelligence, God, who has shared his kingdom with creation, which is ever evolving toward greater Being. We are here to realize our divine potential, the Christ Self within, and to manifest that potential by bringing the kingdom to earth as it is in heaven.

In the following chapters, we shall examine the evidence abounding in the world around us in support of this fourth world view theory. Through the consonance of the earth's revealed religions; through the explorations of psychology and the boundaries of current science; through a clearer understanding of the function of death and the meaning of life; through breakthroughs in healing; through an evolving view of economics to a sense of pervasive world service; we will chart humanity's progress from chaos to its current poise on the threshold of cosmic beauty attainable by the willing of our unified being.

*Within the Western world, there are, of course, many other significant metaphysical and religious groups of believers that are not separately included here, such as Judaism, and Religious Humanism, both of which place perhaps the greatest emphasis on individual morality. It is my best understanding, however, that most of those belief systems not mentioned separately would largely be made up of parts of those world views described above. Also, I have included what I feel to be the main currents of belief and I am quite aware that, indeed, there are many beliefs and world views held by smaller groups or individuals that I have not mentioned.

World Religions

CHAPTER TWO

COMMON THREADS
IN RELIGIOUS SCRIPTURE

"The truth sings its own song and for some mysterious
reason, we are allowed to hear it."
Deepak Chopra, M.D. (quote 113, 116)

In spite of the many differences in both the myths and
practices of the major religions of the world, it is inevitable
for the student of comparative religion to find therein profound commonalities concerning the nature of God, that
which is good and redeeming in life, and the nature of reality
itself. This chapter will explore a few of the commonalities
found in the scriptures and in the writings of major figures of
these seemingly disparate religions.

• • •

HINDUISM
p16

In the Hindu text *The Upanishads*, Brahman is the name
of the Supreme God. Brahman is the Source and end of all,
the Unmanifest Source of all manifestation, the eternal
among things that pass away, the pure consciousness of
conscious being. In Hindu scriptures, creation is described

with many metaphors, such as: "As the wind, though one, takes new forms in whatever it enters, the Spirit, though one, takes new forms in all things that live. He is within all, and is also outside." Brahman is both immanent and transcendent. *The Upanishads* also suggest that we can know God because although God is "an incorporeal Spirit, he can be seen by a heart which is pure ... He is God, the God of love ...."

The manifestion of Brahman is Atman, the eternal individual Self. In *The Upanishads* the Atman is described as the "Spirit of Vision, [which] is never born and never dies. Before him there was nothing, and He is One forevermore." It is also written that "concealed in the heart of all beings is the Atman, the Spirit, the Self; smaller than the smallest atom, greater than the vast spaces."

Also in Hindu scriptures, there is the admonition that the knowledge that we are one with God (Brahman) and with each other is essential to our own happiness. "Who sees all beings in his own Self, and his own Self in all beings, loses all fear," and also "... there are not many, but only One. Who sees variety and not the unity wanders on from death to death."[3]

•   •   •

CHRISTIANITY

One cannot help but note when reading the Beatitudes in the New Testament that the phrase "Blessed are the pure in heart, for they shall see God," reflects the phrase from *The Upanishads* that God can only be seen by "a heart that is pure."

That Brahman, or God, is the source of our being is made most clear in the first chapter of the Gospel according to St. John, which sets out the relationship between God and man explicitly.

In the beginning was the Word, and the Word was with God, and the Word was God.

All things were made by Him; and without Him was not anything made that was made.

In Him was life; and the life was the light of man.

Jesus spoke of the oneness of humankind with each other as well as with God when he said in John 15 "I am in my Father, and ye in me, and I in you." Paul emphasized the immanence and transcendence of God in this passage from Ephesians: "There is one body, and one Spirit, even as ye are called in one hope of your calling: One Lord, one faith, one baptism, one God and Father of all, who is above all, and through all, and in you all" (4:4-6). Elsewhere in scripture we read "Know ye not that you are the temple of God, and that the Spirit of God Dwelleth in you?" (I, Cor: 3:16).

John taught that the way to realize the oneness of God was through love. "And we have known and believed the love that God hath to us. God is love; and he that dwelleth in love dwelleth in God, and God in him" (John 4:16).

There is a glorious passage from the writings of Hildegard of Bingen, the great 12th century Christian mystic, in which God speaks through her, echoing what we have learned about both Hinduism and Christianity, "I, the highest and fiery power, have kindled every living spark and I have breathed out nothing that can die. I flame above the beauty of the fields, I shine in the waters; in the sun, the moon and the stars, I burn … All living things take their radiance from me, and I am the life which remains the same through eternity, having neither beginning nor end." [4]

•   •   •

JUDAISM

Judaism, describing the Creation in the book of Genesis, is explicit in revealing that man partakes of the nature of

God, for it claims that humankind was made in His image and likeness.

> In the beginning God created the Heaven and the earth.
> And the earth was without form, and void; and darkness was upon the face of the deep. And the Spirit of God moved upon the face of the waters.
> And God said, Let there be light: and there was light ....
> And God said, let us make man in our image, after our likeness ....
> So God Created man in his own image, in the image of God Created He him ....

Moses de Leon, a Jewish mystic, expressed his revelation about the oneness of all creation and both the immanence and transcendence of God. "Everything is linked with everything else down to the lowest ring on the chain, and the true essence of God is above as well as below, in the heavens and on the earth, and nothing exists outside Him."[5]

Every religion has its own wording of the Golden Rule. Judaism's version from the Talmud is: "What is bad to you, do not to others. That is the entire Law; all the rest is commentary." "Thou shalt love thy neighbor as thyself" is considered by many the greatest principle of the Torah.

• • •

BUDDHISM

Although the teachings of Prince Guatama, the Buddha, were almost exclusively directed toward the "how" of things (direction for spiritual attainment that would negate a return to the wheel of life and inevitable suffering), there are passages from Buddhist thought which give insight into the nature of the Supreme and the relationship of the Supreme to humankind. "There is an Unborn, Unoriginated, Uncreated, Unformed. If there were not [then] escape from the world of the born, the originated, the created, the form, would not be possible."[6]

Of humankind, Buddhism says, "What is meant by the soul as suchness is the oneness of the totality of things, the great all-including whole, the quintessence of the doctrine, for the essential nature of the soul is uncreated and eternal." Also in Buddhist writings, we find reminders of the necessity that humankind understands its relationship to the Creator and all His creation. "When the oneness of the totality of things is not recognized, then ignorance as well as particularization arises, and all phases of the defiled mind are thus developed."[7]

Buddhist practice includes the cultivation of four qualities said to be divine conditions of the mind: compassion, loving-kindness, sympathetic joy, and equanimity. Described as the Compassionate Buddha, it is natural that Gautama's teachings would emphasize love, and would describe happiness as, "Full of love for all things in the world, practicing virtue in order to benefit others, this man alone is happy." Buddhism also teaches, "He that loveth not, knoweth not God. For God is love."[8]

• • •

ISLAM

The greatest part of the Qu'ran of Islam consists of directions for living and moral prescriptions. However, what is mentioned of the nature of God and humankind is revealing. Muslims are told to believe and to say "He is one God, one, God the ever self-sufficing, He begets not, nor is begotten. None is like unto Him."[9] Of humankind the Qu'ran says, "On God's own nature has been molded man's." It is written in *The Hadith* that Muhammad said "He who knows his own self knows God." Islam teaches that "All creatures are the family of God, and he is the most beloved of God who does most good unto His family."[10]

Neil Douglas-Klotz, in a translation of, and meditation on, a passage from the Qu'ran, Sura 112, illumines the concept of oneness or unity as expressed in Islam.

> Ultimate Unity throughout the cosmos envelopes
> and surrounds all dimensions, measurements, laws
> and tendencies. It fulfills and completes all potentials
> that unfold in joy throughout the Universe.
> Unity is the eternal Now—
> nothing is born from it and nothing produces it.
> It is the seed of both cause and effect.

To the Sufi sect of Islam belong most of the great Muslim mystics. The following is by Rumi, perhaps Islam's most beloved poet.

> There is a force within that gives you life—
> seek that.
> In your body there lies a priceless jewel—
> seek that.
> Oh, wandering Sufi,
> If you are in search of the greatest treasure,
> don't look outside,
> Look within, and seek That.

• • •

TAOISM

The Tao of Taoism may be translated as the "Way" and also as the "Source of the Way." Laotse, who gave the original teaching, was simply a man who had become one with the Way; he did not claim individual divinity. It is important to note that the Way of Taoism is not the traditional path to "something." It *is* the ultimate "something," as well as the ultimate Source. If you are "in the Tao," you are walking in the light of truth; your life, in tune with the natural order of things, flourishes.

Taoism is very similar to Hinduism in its poetic explanation of the unexplainable.

> There is a thing inherent and natural,
> Which existed before heaven and earth.
> Motionless and fathomless,
> It stands alone and never changes;
> It pervades everywhere and never becomes
> exhausted.
> It may be regarded as the Mother of the
> Universe
>
> I do not know its name.
> If I am forced to give it a name,
> I call it Tao, and I name it as Supreme ...[11]

"Your self," it is written in *The Wisdom of Laotse* "is a body lent to you by the universe. Your life is not possessed by you; it is a harmony lent to you by the universe. Your nature is not possessed by you; it is a natural evolution lent to you by the universe."[12] This text makes it clear that the ability to achieve harmony with the universal principle or Tao is innate in all men. The Oneness of all is emphasized in Taoist teachings, but perhaps most dramatically in the following statement: "We are embraced in the obliterating unity of God."[13]

Humility and selflessness are highly prized qualities in Taoism. It is also written in Taoist scripture that "To love one's fellowman and benefit all is called humanity," associating giving love with being human.[14]

•   •   •

BAHA'I

The religion of Baha'i, meaning the followers of Baha'u'llah, is the latest in a long line of revealed religions. In fact, it was part of Baha'u'llah's teaching that the messengers of God are "agents of a single, unbroken process, the awakening of the human race to its spiritual and moral potentialities."[15] Baha'u'llah saw himself as one among many teachers all connected through a single purpose. In particular, he followed the footsteps of Moses, Jesus and Muhammad, in a process of progressive revelations—each with a definite mission and message suited to the needs of the times and the cultural and psychological stage of the people. According to Baha'u'llah, "the sequence of the divine Revelations is a process that hath no beginning and will have no end. Their messages are an integral part of an ongoing and progressive unfoldment of God's power and will."[16]

The nature of God, according to the teachings of the Baha'is, is both transcendent and immanent, as we have seen is the case with the other revelations we have examined. Speaking of the one true God, Baha'u'llah teaches: "This is the Ocean out of which all seas have proceeded, and with which every one of them will ultimately be united. From Him all the Suns have been generated, and unto Him they will all return."[17] Of the transcendence of God, he teaches: "The whole universe reflecteth his glory, while He is Himself independent of, and transcendeth His creatures."[18]

According to these teachings, it is the nature of humankind to reflect the nature of God. In the following passages, through Baha'u'llah, God reveals this truth: "With the hands of power I made thee and with the fingers of strength I created thee; and within thee have I placed the essence of My light." Another revealing passage claims, "He that hath known God hath known himself."

Baha'u'llah teaches, however, that humankind has free will to choose to express its God nature or not. According to the Baha'i scriptures, it is up to the volition of each individual to express and manifest his or her divine potential. It is toward the evolutionary process which will bring humanity to a full expression of this potential that the revelations of God are directed. The purpose of the teachings of the prophets, Baha'u'llah says, is that "the whole human race can be illumined with the light of unity, and the remembrance of His Name is able to set on fire the hearts of all men, and burn away the veils that intervene between them and His glory."[19]

Not only is humankind in essence one with God, he is also one with his fellowmen. More than any other revealed religion, Baha'i teaches the unity of humankind. According to Baha'u'llah's teachings, paradoxically, it is "only by achieving true unity that humanity can fully cultivate its diversity and individuality. This is the stage to which all Manifestations [prophets] have been working and is the stage upon which humanity is now entering."[20]

The manifestation of love is absolutely necessary to the coming of the realization of innate unity among all people. We find in Bahai the following scripture: "The brightness and fire of your love will no doubt fuse and unify the contending peoples and kindred of the earth." Also, "the fundamental purpose animating the Faith of God and His Religion is to safeguard the interest and promote the unity of the human race, and to foster the spirit of love and fellowship amongst men."[21]

•   •   •

Through a brief examination of the philosophies of the above major religions, we have found many commonalities of belief, which are also among the basic tenets of the Perennial Philosophy. There is one God and one Creator. God is Spirit, God is love, God is Intelligence, God is Supreme, and man was created in His image and likeness. All Creation is one in God, Who is both transcendent and immanent. We realize this oneness through love, which is the underlying force and foundation of all manifestation. When that magnificent truth seeps into the deepest recesses of man's consciousness, humankind will begin to experience its destiny. Perhaps there will be a dawning of the Age of Aquarius, when "peace will guide the planets and love will steer the stars."

*Although the Hindu religion seemingly has many gods, all are considered different manifestations of the one God or Brahman.

CHAPTER THREE

INSIGHTS FROM PSYCHOLOGY

"What lies behind us and what lies before us are tiny
matters compared to what lies within us."
Oliver Wendell Holmes

Psychology has as its field of study the mind, consciousness, and the behavior of the human being. As we explore a
major train of development in psychological theory we will
find that the deepest insights of the major religious traditions
concerning the nature of humankind are supported by
prominent schools of psychology.

Psychology, itself a very young science, has its roots in
the British Empiricism of John Locke and David Hume. With
the work of Freud, psychology began to develop more fully in
Austria and Germany, followed by an intensification of
psychological practice and study in the United States. In
general, the psychological theories and advances which have
had the largest impact on current psychological theory and in
which I see an important progression are: Freud's discovery
of the subconscious and his development of psychoanalytic
theory; Behaviorism, as developed mainly by John B. Watson
and B. F. Skinner; the school of Jungian thought, which has
been a forerunner of Humanistic Psychology; and finally,

Transpersonal Psychology, an offshoot of the Humanistic School as well as the work of Abraham Maslow and Roberto Assagioli, among others. *Opn*

The progression of psychological thought through these different theories and schools seems to present pieces of a vast puzzle which are beginning to form a picture of human nature. This gathering knowledge is giving us an idea of who we are, both as a present reality as well as our potential for change and transcendence. As psychology has progressed, the difficulty is that oftentimes, as psychologists are caught up with the excitement of a new insight into human nature, the part has been taken for the whole.

•   •   •

Society owes a great debt to Sigmund Freud for the greater understanding of our mental processes that came with his recognition of the subconscious. Also, Freud's related development of the psychological therapy of psycho-analysis provided much corroborative material. Freud came to believe that the primary motivations affecting people are the desires for power and sexual pleasure, and the avoidance of pain. People, driven by these sexual and power needs, were required by society's mores to compromise in obtaining grat-ification. Therefore, many of these needs were repressed, usually in childhood. Freud felt the mental states of most people were circumscribed by repressed desires and sexual urges; at best, most developed mental blocks, and at worst, neuroses and psychoses.

Jung and Adler, two of Freud's most notable associates, both left in protest of Freud's insistence on the prime impor-tance of infant sexuality and the Oedipus Complex. However, the basic structure of Freud's psychoanalytic theory is still in use today, even though there is disagreement on the emphasis to be awarded various Freudian theories.

Freud's view of human nature was very dim indeed. The

goal of his therapy was to help his patients adapt to a world devoid of inherent spirituality or values. However, within this context, he did try to help people remove psychological obstacles to a higher level of functioning. Moreover, Freud gave us invaluable insights into human nature, for we do suffer from repressions, blocks, and neuroses. It is interesting to note that Freud himself may have had doubts that his theory was balanced and complete. He remarked toward the end of his life "If I had my life to live over, I would devote myself to psychical research rather than psychoanalysis."[22]

•　　•　　•

The psychological school of Behaviorism, introduced by J. B. Watson and further developed by B. F. Skinner, explains behavior as entirely a psychological response to environmental stimuli. Watson denied the value of introspection, rejecting consciousness as an unscientific concept. He believed that psychology should be strictly a study of observable phenomena. This theory posited that all behavior can be modeled and shaped through conditioning and learning. One of the favorite claims of behaviorists is that they can take any baby and make any kind of person of him/her.

The Behaviorist school of thought has afforded us great advances in understanding behavior. Undoubtedly we are all conditioned from birth: by our family, our culture—which includes such sub-cultures as race, socio-economic group, place (city, state, nation)—our occupation, our language and our own unique experiences. In *The Reality Illusion*, Ralph Strauch asserts that our experience consists of two components: events and interpretation of events. Through our conditioning, which affects our interpretation of events, we develop habitual patterns of behavior operating below the level of conscious choice.

In order to show how powerfully the forces of culture and society shape our world, the prominent sociologist, Milhaly

Csikszentmihaly, in his brilliant book *The Evolving Self: A Psychology for the Third Millennium*, explains: "As people interact with parents, friends, and co-workers, they learn to see the world from the vantage point of those particular interactions. The world looks very different from a business men's club than from a union hall, a military barracks, or a monastery .... People in different positions in the social system end up living in different physical and symbolic environments—in what are, in effect, alien worlds."[23]

No doubt the study of conditioning and learned behavior has advanced our study of human nature. The more we know about ourselves, the better, and to know that we have been conditioned by certain circumstances is to set us free in a real sense to enjoy and act in a larger world. It is not to deny conditioning and learned behavior that we take exception with the Behavioristic School of Psychology. It is the denial of the relevance of other parts of our nature that is hurtful to the complete understanding of ourselves. Our own intuitions about ourselves tell us that we are more than instinctual urges, and more than our conditioning. Aldous Huxley's *Brave New World* dramatized that people can be controlled and conditioned, but the spirit of humankind cannot be eliminated. And as Ralph Strauch says, "Our barriers to direct awareness are not fixed and immutable from birth. To a large extent, they are learned and they can be unlearned."[24]

New schools of psychology have built upon and used the important information from Freudian and behavioristic theory, and have gone ahead to forge a new picture of human nature. Among the most prominent of the new roads forged in psychological thought are Jungian (the work of Carl Jung), Humanistic, and Transpersonal Psychology.

• • •

Carl Gustav Jung, a native of Switzerland, has made a powerful impact both on the science of psychology and clinical methods used in therapy. His influence is growing, as evidenced by "The Friends of Jung" groups popping up around the United States. As previously mentioned, Jung broke off his association with Freud because he differed with his extreme emphasis on sexuality as the root of most psychological problems. Jung went on to develop a body of psychological thought that was original in many ways, while building on Freud's psychoanalytic theory.

Ultimately, Jung saw the unconscious as having two systems: the personal, which harbored the repressed events of the personal life; and the collective unconscious, where archetypes were found—universal patterns or prototypes of things, and where experiences and inherited tendencies developed throughout the evolution of humankind. Jung believed that it was through working with the collective unconscious in therapy that the human being could transcend the personal self, with its repressed fears and desires, and become his or her true individualized Self. According to Jung this transcendence can happen when the active imagination, through therapy, engages the archetypes and images of the unconscious. The realization of a "new self" can then arise, experienced as being the personal self, and yet more than that—both personal and transcendent.

That most people do not know who they really are was central to Jung's theories. As he wrote in *The Undiscovered Self*, "most people confuse 'self-knowledge' with knowledge of their conscious ego personalities. Anyone who has ego-consciousness at all takes it for granted that he knows himself. But the ego knows only its own contents, not the unconscious and its contents …. What is called 'self-knowledge' is therefore very limited knowledge, most of it dependent on social factors, or what goes on in the human psyche."[25] The Self to Jung is the true center and totality of a person, the original wholeness out of which the personality is formed, whereas the ego is merely the center of personal consciousness. The ego creates division; the Self promotes unity and wholeness. Jung once called psychiatry "the art of healing the soul."

Jung's religious views were grounded in mystical consciousness. He wrote, "The seat of faith ... is not consciousness but spontaneous religious experience, which brings the individual's faith into immediate relation with God."[26] Jung argues, "That religious experiences exist no longer needs proof. But it will always remain doubtful whether what metaphysics and theology call God and the gods is the real ground of these experiences." However, he goes on to say, "Anyone who has had it is seized by it and therefore not in a position to indulge in fruitless metaphysical or epistemological speculations. Absolute certainty brings its own evidence and has not need of anthropomorphic proofs."[27] Once when Jung was asked if he believed in God he replied that he did not need to believe; he knew.

With Jung, psychological thought has come a long way from the view of humans as merely bundles of blocks, repressions, and neuroses, or merely conditioned automatons. Jung's view of humanity shows the way for us to transcend our lower self and become a Higher Self, whole and free. His theories and practices profoundly influenced the direction of psychological thought and were influential in bringing about the school of Humanistic Psychology, as well as Transpersonal Psychology.

• • •

In many ways, Humanistic Psychology was a reaction against behaviorism. Those who developed it believed that the study of mind and personality is not amenable to the same kinds of scientific methods used in studying animals. Nor is human nature completely defined by behavioristic views of the preeminence of conditioning in determining behavior. In humanistic theory each individual is responsible for his or her own personal development, and for finding a moral code and set of values to give life meaning. Such an endeavor would involve coming to an understanding of what parts of our personality have been conditioned, and what blocks and repressions exist in our subconscious, in order to free the individual for self-determination.

Although Adler, Allport, Carl Rogers and Jung were forerunners of Humanistic Psychology, it was Abraham Maslow who developed it most completely and who also figured largely in the later development of Transpersonal Psychology. Maslow was disturbed by the trend in psychology to define humankind by its pathology, and thus he undertook a study of mentally and emotionally healthy people. What he found has led the way to a new vision of human nature in the field of psychology.

After identifying, through a well-defined study, a group of mentally and emotionally healthy people and the values they exhibited, Maslow termed them "self-actualizers." Self-actualizers exhibit B (being) Values, outlined in full in his *Toward a Psychology of Being*. Maslow describes "'self-actualizing people' as those who have come to a high level of maturation, health, and self-fulfillment, [and who] have so much to teach us that sometimes they seem almost like a different breed of human beings."[28] Another description of self-actualizers sounds very much like prescriptions coming from the highest religious wisdom. "My [Maslow's] findings indicate that in the normal perceptions of self-actualizing people and in the more occasional peak experiences of average people, perception can be relatively ego-transcending, self-forgetful, egoless. It can be unmotivated, impersonal, desireless, unselfish, not needing, detached."[29] Maslow also discovered that self-actualizers tended to have a high incidence of what he termed "peak-experiences" (secularized religious, mystical, or transcendental experiences). Maslow claims that "peakers" find these experiences self-validating, that in fact they are "so valuable that they make life worthwhile by their occasional occurrence."[30] Maslow also found from this extensive study that "the world seen in peak-experiences is seen only as beautiful, good, desirable, worthwhile, etc., and is never experienced as evil or undesirable."[31] Life is reacted to with awe, wonder, amazement, humility and even reverence, exaltation and piety. It was these findings that led Maslow into the realm of transpersonal psychology.**

•   •   •

The roots of transpersonal psychology may be traced back to William James, who explored states of higher consciousness in his classic book *The Varieties of Religious Experience*. Jung contributed to the movement with his idea that the concept of individuation transcended the personal, and with his vision of a Higher Self. Abraham Maslow's work exploring the higher reaches of human nature, as well as his documentation of "peak" experiences of self-actualized persons, began this work in earnest. There have been many other important contributions to the school of transpersonal psychology by many well known psychologists and psychiatrists. I will focus on Roberto Assagioli and his development of Psychosynthesis, which I believe to be one of the definitive works in this field.

Transpersonal Psychology, along with Humanistic Psychology, works toward the full realization of human possibilities. Transpersonal Psychology also aims toward the awakening, release and use of potent supraconscious spiritual energies that may be reached through direct experience of the Self. This recognition of the spiritual dimension of a person is not necessary to the practice of Humanistic Psychology.

Psychology has long realized that an individual existential crisis is often responsible for depression, and many other psychological problems that bring people to the therapy couch. Transpersonal Psychology sees this crisis as a positive event that can lead to a leap forward in both personal function and spiritual growth. According to Seymoor Boorstein in *Transpersonal Psychology:* "The existential crisis is a crisis in which the very basis of individual existence—an existence which had been unfolding primarily along the personal dimension—comes into question ... [the] resolution is found when the individual is able to expand the meaning of his existence beyond the boundaries of his own personality in order to purposefully participate in the life of the whole."[32]

Roberto Assagioli (1888-1974) believed the existence of a spiritual Self and of a superconscious are as basic to human nature as the instinctive energies described by Freud. Assagioli, like many of his contemporaries, began his studies of psychology and psychiatry with Freud. He also studied with and was influenced by Carl Jung and Abraham Maslow, who introduced him to the concepts of self-actualization, self-realization and the will-to-grow. In 1926, Assagioli founded the Institute of Psychic Culture and Therapy in Rome, which was later renamed the Psychosynthesis Institute.

According to Assagioli "the underlying strengths of Psychosynthesis are its eclectic and holistic approach, its open and non-dogmatic attitude, its recognition of the spiritual nature of humanity and the central role played by the superconscious and the will in fashioning human destiny."[33] Central to Assagioli's theory and practice is the importance of recognizing "the difference that exists between the Self in its essential nature and the small ordinary personality, the little self or ego, of which we are normally conscious."[34] Psychosynthesis actually means the formation or reconstruction of the personality around a new center.

The therapy developed by Assagioli as part of the complete system provides the means to make this transition. First comes the integration of the personality around the conscious self. This, however, is a step toward the final integration or union with the Higher Self. Put more poetically,

"Psychosynthesis undertakes the great work of transforming human life into a true work of art, into a fit dwelling place for the Divine Spark."[35]

In fact, it has been said that Psychosynthesis is really the reappearance in the modern world of the perennial philosophy, associated with the wisdom of the ancients. Peter deCoppens, in a discussion of Assagioli's work, makes the striking comparison of the ancient injunction associated with the perennial philosophy—"Oh, Man, Know Thyself. Be the Master of Thyself, Seek Harmony with Thyself. Become Thy Higher Self," with the motto of Assagioli's psychosynthesis—"Oh Man, Know Thyself, Possess Thyself, Transform Thyself, Realize Thy Higher self."[36]

Assagioli's own words sum up most profoundly how transpersonal psychology parallels the wisdom we find in the perennial philosophy and throughout the major religions that directs us toward transcendence.***

> ... universal life itself appears to us as a struggle between multiplicity and unity—a labor and an aspiration towards union. We seem to sense that—whether we conceive it as a divine Being or as cosmic energy—the Spirit working upon and within all creation is shaping it into order, harmony, and beauty, uniting all beings (some willing but the majority as yet blind and rebellious) with each other through links of love, achieving—slowly and silently, but powerfully and irresistibly—the Supreme Synthesis.[37]

• • •

*Obviously, there have been many other schools of psychological thought and contributions to the field. The above cited are the major developments as I interpret them.

**Maslow's complete philosophy and findings on self-actu-
alizers and "peakers" may be found in his books *THE
FARTHER REACHES OF HUMAN NATURE* and
TOWARD A PSYCHOLOGY OF BEING.

***It would be interesting for readers to note how close the
spirit of this quotation is to the work of Teilhard de
Chardin.

SECTION II:
FROM THE UNREAL TO THE REAL

This we know, all things are connected like the blood which unites one family. All things are connected. Whatever befalls the Earth, befalls the sons of the Earth. Man did not weave the web of life; he is merely a strand in it. Whatever he does to the web, he does to himself.
Chief Seattle

The dominant world views of the past have provided the knowledge and impetus which have guided humanity in many positive directions, and have brought about great advancements in government, technology and the arts. Why, then, are we floundering on the edge of chaos? Because as productive as past world views have been, they provided only a partial "map of the territory." They have not provided crucial information about ourselves and our world, and have thus led us down some very destructive paths.

Whereas in many past and even current world views the physical world was understood to be solid and particular, we now know it is fluid and connected. In the same way, the human entity has been thought to be one of many particular individuals. We are now beginning to realize that each person is a part of all humanity as a wave is part of the ocean. With this knowledge comes the realization that our ancient win/lose ways of solving problems are anathema not only to our survival but to our happiness as well.

Other myths about human nature have added to the dilemma in which we find ourselves. Since the ending of pre-history the masculine sex has been deemed superior, elevated in status, with more opportunity to realize innate potential. The feminine sex, relegated to inferior status, has been largely denied the opportunity to develop and thus contribute fully to society. From our new understanding of human nature, we know that only with a balanced flourishing of masculine and feminine qualities can we have a full flowering of humanity's potential.

CHAPTER FOUR

PHYSICS,
GENERAL SYSTEMS THEORY,
AND THE SCIENCE OF CHAOS:
AN UNFOLDING DRAMA

As it is with light and electricity, so it may be with life;
the phenomena may be individuals carrying on separate existences in space and time, while in the deeper
reality beyond space and time we may all be members of the same body.

Sir James Jeans, physicist

An exciting scientific drama has been playing out in the
20th century that gives us further insight into the nature of
reality, the world and our place in it, and the curtain has not
fallen. The discoveries that led to the classification of
quantum physics were formulated over a period of three
decades by an international group of physicists working
together across national borders to shape one of the most
exciting periods of modern science. In developing quantum
theory they overturned a scientific paradigm that had been in
place for several hundred years. These physicists themselves
were continually stunned and baffled by their findings. Neils
Bohr, one of the founding fathers of quantum physics, said

"no one knows how it can be this way."

The implications of quantum theory are profound and are opening new vistas of metaphysical speculation, while also offering a substantial background for a new acceptance and understanding of the perennial philosophy.

In fact, some physicists believe that quantum theory will lead to the unification of physics with metaphysics, representing two sides of one coin.

Quantum theory is not easily understood, offering considerable challenge to the lay person. The following narrative highlights the major developments of the quantum drama, and seeks to make clear its nature as an essential underpinning of the ancient, but still new, perennial philosophy.

To better understand the way in which quantum theory has overturned the previous time-honored views of physics, it is important to see it in the perspective of the "old" Newtonian paradigm.

Rene Descartes and Isaac Newton were, among many other players, the "stars" of the drama entitled "Scientific Realism," sometimes called "Materialism," that first came on the scene in the 17th century. Descartes hypothesized that the world might be a machine—like an automaton—created by God and set in motion to run forever according to certain laws. However, because Descartes was a very religious man, this view did not completely satisfy him, and in modification of it, he developed a theory that haunts us yet—the philosophy of *dualism*, which divided the world into one sphere of matter and another sphere of mind. Science would be the objective domain of matter, and religion, which is subjective, would be the domain of mind. Thus were matter and mind seemingly irrevocably separated, as were science and religion.

Isaac Newton developed theories that reinforced the notion of the world as a Grand Machine. Newton established "that all motion can be predicted exactly given the laws of motion and the initial conditions of the objects [their starting point and initial impetus]." In other words, Newton established *causal determinism.*

In the larger world that we feel, taste, touch, smell, and see—the macro world—the theories of Descartes and Newton were responsible for great strides made by science in predicting and controlling the environment, bringing to humanity many wonderful technologies. In fact, the material aspect of Descartes' theory worked so well, that the scientific world began to question the other half of his theory—the subjective world of mind. Thus the principle of *material monism* was added to the list of postulates of material realism, alleging that all things in the world, including mind and consciousness, are made of matter. The derivative conclusion of this theory was that consciousness became a property of the brain and could be explained by material phenomena only.

These theories led to what is known as "reductionism" in the practice of science. It was virtually universally accepted that complex phenomena could always be understood by reducing them to their basic building blocks and then looking for the mechanism through which these interacted. Physicist, Amit Goswami, sums up in *THE SELF AWARE UNIVERSE*, the five principles of the philosophy of material realism:

1. **Strong objectivity:** Objects are independent of and separate from the mind or consciousness.

2. **Causal determinism:** All motion can be predicted exactly given the laws of motion and the initial conditions of the objects, (where they are and with what velocity they are moving).

3. **Physical or material realism:** (Often called materialism): All is made of matter.

4. **Epiphenomenalism:** All mental phenomena can be explained as a secondary phenomena of matter by a suitable reduction to antecedent physical conditions.

5. *Locality:* The highest velocity is that of light, therefore all influence, or interactions between material objects, are mediated via local signals. In other words no material object can be influenced by anything that travels faster than light because that is impossible within the confines of our universe.[38]

•   •   •

THE PLAYERS IN THE COSMIC DRAMA OF QUANTUM PHYSICS

MAX PLANCK: (Nobel Prize in Physics, 1918) Max Planck, German physicist, is the recognized father of quantum theory. He discovered that energy is not given off continuously, but in the form of individual units, called quanta—a discovery that ushered in the entire quantum revolution.

ALBERT EINSTEIN: (Nobel Prize in Physics, 1921) Parts of Einstein's relativity theory provided impetus and background for the development of quantum theory: his explanation of the photoelectric effect in terms of light quanta, challenging the classical view of light appearing only as waves; the discovery that mass and energy are equivalent, that mass is a form of energy and vice versa, and that the observations of space and time are not independent of the observer. These revelations changed the direction of physics, providing the world with a totally different view of nature—we now saw a physical reality composed of interactive energy states. Physicists could no longer talk of space and time, but only of space/time.

LOUIS DE BROGLIE: (Nobel Prize in Physics, 1929) Through an analogy with the sound waves of a guitar, French physicist Louis De Broglie developed the theory of matter waves—which posited that moving electrons produce waves. In his thesis, De Broglie postulated that all matter behaves as both a particle and a wave. Wave characteristics, however, are detectable only at the atomic level, whereas the classical (Newtonian) properties of matter are apparent at larger scales. His work had a direct effect on that of Erwin Schroedinger.

ERWIN SCHROEDINGER: (Nobel Prize in Physics, 1933) In the 1920s Schroedinger used the work of De Broglie to develop his own theory of wave mechanics. Their combined work put together another important piece of the puzzle of quantum physics, definitely establishing the existence of matter/waves—which had a direct effect upon the work of Werner Heisenberg and his associates.

WERNER HEISENBERG: (Nobel Prize in Physics, 1932) In 1925 Heisenberg, with others, formulated the Uncertainty Principle, which combined with Erwin Schroedinger's wave equation, brought about the formation of modern quantum mechanics, a division of quantum physics. The Uncertainty Principle, along with the developments that led up to it, has had a revolutionary effect upon the principles of classical physics. It states that although as a particle a given entity is localized, its wave nature makes its location within a particular atom impossible to determine with certainty; it remains a probability only. It is possible to establish either the position of a particle or its velocity and momentum, but not both. In other words, it is impossible to know at any one moment if a given bit of matter is acting as a particle or a wave. This principle has amazing implications for our understanding of the nature of reality.

NEILS BOHR: (Nobel Prize in Physics, 1922) The Danish physicist Neils Bohr is also considered one of the founding fathers of quantum mechanics. In his work with light, Bohr was able to explain in terms of quanta how atoms absorb and radiate energy. Also important to quantum theory, is Bohr's concept of complementarity to explain the wave-particle duality put forth by Heisenberg's Uncertainty Principle. This concept suggests that this uncertainty is not part of the particle's behavior but results from the physicist's interaction with them.

The new quantum theory was now calling into question the classical principle of causal determinism, since matter must now be considered an indeterminate interplay of energies. It questioned the principle of locality as well since that depended on the causal nature of *local* variables, or matter acting in space in predictable ways. Some physicists, including Einstein, took exception to these implications of quantum mechanics, feeling that there must be variables not yet known that would resolve these very unsatisfying questions about reality. Einstein summed up his position in the famous quotation: "God does not play dice with the Universe."

JOHN S. BELL: Interested in the controversy over non-local causality, John Bell worked out a mathematical proof of a non-causal connection of elements distant from each other, known as Bell's Theorem—positing that the idea of local hidden variables is not compatible with quantum mechanics. In Bell's mathematical proof, these non-causal, non-local connections are instantaneous, involving no signals between particles. Although Bell's Theorem caught the attention of many physicists, it wasn't until Alain Aspect worked out the experiment that would give it proof that it became more universally accepted.

ALAIN ASPECT: Alain Aspect's experiment verified that there is signal-less (no contact) influence operating between two correlated quantum objects by proving that "a measurement of one photon affects its polarization-correlated partner without any exchange of local signals between them."[39] His experiment thus established non-locality in quantum mechanics. To put this in more simple terms, it showed that when two particles have interacted and are then separated, if one of the particles is subsequently acted upon or influenced in some way, the other particle will instantaneously react.

The basic premises of classical Newtonian physics are all directly challenged as a result of the discoveries documented above.

STRONG OBJECTIVITY: We have seen that Heisenberg's Uncertainty Principle has more than challenged the concept that there is an objective material world quite separate from and independent of human observers. We now know, on a microscopic level, what we cannot know. We cannot know in advance whether a quantum object is a wave or a particle; we can only know probabilities. The very act of measuring participates in the result, or as physicists say, "collapses the quantum wave packet to a localized particle" and "subject and objects are inextricably blended together." Or, as Fritjof Capra explains, "The discovery of the dual aspect of matter and of the fundamental role of probability has demolished the classical notion of solid objects. At the subatomic level, the solid material objects of classical physics dissolve into wavelike patterns of probabilities."[40]

CAUSAL DETERMINISM: A premise basic to the old physics was that, with the foreknowledge of the initial conditions of the objects being measured, the world is fundamentally deterministic. We now know, however, that a strict cause-effect description of the behavior of a single object is impossible. There is only statistical cause and statistical effect when we talk about a large group of particles. In the microworld, quantum events are not determined absolutely by preceding causes. Although the probability of a given event is fixed by theory, the actual outcome of particular quantum process is unknown. As stated by physicist Paul Davies in *THE MIND OF GOD*, "Heisenberg's Uncertainty Principle puts paid to the notion that the present determines the future exactly."[41]

LOCALITY: As we have seen above, Bell's Theorem and Alain Aspect's proof of it have drawn the curtain on the principle of locality—that all interactions between material objects are mediated via local signals. Bell and Aspect have shown without depending on quantum theory, but only the facts, that there are *instantaneous* non-causal connections of elements distant from each other. This, of course, violates

Einstein's assertion that "no-thing" is able to move faster than light in our universe. Therefore "some-thing" must be operating "outside" our universe. The "hidden variable" that Einstein and others hoped to find that would explain the "uncertainty" of the micro world may exist, but not within the confines of the known universe.

PHYSICAL OR MATERIAL MONISM: MATERI-ALISM: The assumption that reality is completely objective and outside of the observer has been severely called into question by the Uncertainty Principle. In fact, some physicists such as Neils Bohr, believe there is no deep reality at all, or as Bohr states it "There is no quantum world. There is only an abstract description of it." With the very existence of matter at the subatomic level being called into question, a theory that reduces everything to matter, including all states of consciousness and all subjective feelings, appears more than out of date.

EPIPHENOMENALISM: This principle, which postulates that consciousness is, by some undetermined means, a material product of the mind, is directly related to physical realism or materialism. In the context of quantum mechanics, it is an illogical assumption. Physicist Paul Davies suggests that it would be absurd to conclude that an epiphenomenon, or derivative, of matter could affect matter.

The quiet revolution of quantum physics has now put to rest many of the assumptions of Newtonian physics and scientific realism. The world now, according to physicist Nick Herbert, is made entirely of one substance—"quantum-stuff." The old or "Newtonian" physics lives on as a part of the new physics, explaining much of what happens in the macro-world of matter. But a whole new era has dawned; the question of the "nature of reality" that is the realm of physics has been opened for further investigation.*

•   •   •

SYSTEMS THEORY
AND THE SCIENCE OF CHAOS

The surprising revelations of quantum physics about the nature of reality were complemented by theories which were being developed in the areas of general systems and the science of chaos. When taken together, the knowledge that is gained from these disciplines gives verification to ideas long embodied in the perennial philosophy.

General Systems Theory was the outcome of research that biologist Ludwig von Bertalanffy undertook in the 1940s to discover how organisms are able to sustain themselves in their environment. Ultimately he proposed the "open" system model, one that exchanges energy with its environment, as opposed to the "closed" system, modeled on the machine, which will always run down if left unfueled by energy added from without. Bertalanffy defined an open system as being in a constant state of flux, also termed disequilibrium or far-from-equilibrium. A closed system is one in which the useful energy has dissipated away to a state of maximum entropy, or disintegration. General Systems Theory has come to have far reaching effects, in that it requires us to see the world in terms of the interrelatedness and interdependence of all phenomena.

Several decades after Bertalanffy's contribution, Ilya Prigogine, a Russian-born Belgian, received a Nobel Prize for chemistry for work that furthered the understanding of systems theory. Through his study of thermodynamics, Prigogine found that although in closed systems entropy, and therefore disorder, must increase owing to irreversible processes, open systems, which exchange matter with their environment, can advance toward increasing differentiation and organization, as is the case in the development and evolution of biological phenomena.

Through his work with chemicals, Prigogine developed the theory of "dissipative structures," a system in a far-from-equilibrium state. The act of the system exchanging energy with its environment can result in fluctuations. If the disturbance is intense, the system can reach a "bifurcation point," at which time it is possible for the system to undergo a reordering on a higher level. It is impossible to know in advance, however, whether the system will reorder on a higher level or whether it will disintegrate into chaos.

Even if the system goes toward chaos, an inherent order usually will emerge. Prigogine showed, according to Capra, that "dissipative structures display the dynamics of self-organization in its simplest form, exhibiting most of the phenomena characteristic of life-self renewal, adaptation, evolution and even primitive forms of mental processes." In far-from-equilibrium states, it was discovered, systems do not break down. Instead, new systems emerge. Prigogine's theory suggests that evolution is a natural response to crisis.

General Systems Theory gave rise to what is now called the Science of Complexity, which studies the development and functioning of complex systems. Along with the study of complexity came the new field of Chaos Science.

Chaos Science is a curious world of solitons, fractals, and strange attractors. I have given an optimistic implication of chaos study at the beginning of this book—that order is inherent in chaos. It is from chaos that order arises. When a system reaches a state of turbulence due to perturbation from interactions with its environment, chaos churns away from order, only to reorder in a more complex and often more useful fashion, drawn by what chaos theory calls "strange attractors." (Perhaps these "attractors" are called "strange" because no one really knows what they are. It has been suggested that they might embody the pull of "meaning" that draws life ever onward.)

The science of chaos is changing our view of reality, how we perceive the world and its meaning. John Briggs and F. David Peat, in *Turbulent Mirror: An Illustrated Guide to Chaos and the Science of Wholeness*, state that: 1989

… scientists are showing how the strange laws of chaos lie behind many if not most of the things we consider remarkable about our world: the human heartbeat and human thoughts, clouds, storms, the structure of galaxies, the creation of a poem, the rise and fall of the gypsy moth population, the spread of a forest fire, a winding coast line, even the origins of life itself.[42]

There are at least five tenets of chaos theory:

1. **The non-equilibrium state is the source of order**
   Prigogine and Stengers explain in their book *Order Out of Chaos*, that nonequilibrium *brings* "order out of chaos." As we have stated earlier, a system is in nonequilibrium when it is exchanging energy with its environment. "In far-from-equilibrium conditions we may have transformation from disorder, from thermal chaos, into order. New dynamic states of matter may originate, states that reflect the interaction of a given system with its surroundings."[43]

2. **All things are interrelated**
   According to chaos scientists Briggs and Peat, "… the evolution of complex systems can't be followed in causal detail because such systems are holistic: everything effects everything else."[44] This tenet relates to all disciplines.

3. **Unpredictableness of nature**
   Although Chaos Theory is based on Newtonian mechanical principles (working in the macro world), in its unpredictability it shares the uncertainty experienced at the quantum level. For instance, the results of the work that Prigogine undertook in chemistry, as well as the work fellow scientist Lorenz was doing in meteorology, were com-

pletely unpredictable. This tenet is related to the next.

4. **Sensitive dependence on initial conditions**
    Meteorologist Edward Lorenz found that a weather system in a different part of the world could be affected by the flap of a butterfly's wings in Tokyo. On a grander scale,

    cosmologists speculate that if the initial conditions at the Big Bang had varied by as much as a single quantum of energy (the smallest known thing we can measure), the universe would be a vastly different place. The whole shape of things depends upon the minutest part. The part is the whole in this respect, for through the action of any part, the whole, in the form of chaos or transformative change, may manifest.[45]

    It is for this reason that chaos researchers emphasize the fifth tenet.

5. **We participate in creating our world through our interaction with the environment:**
    Briggs and Peat write that we are "an integral part of the time-bound, spontaneously organized movement of nature, not a low-probability accident."[46] As we human beings interact with our environment, we are having very definite input into the world that we experience. We actually help shape reality, add meaning to the world, and determine our future.

• • •

David Bohm, one of the world's foremost theoretical physicists, was concerned not only with the fields of quantum theory and relativity, but also their underlying philosophical meaning. His theory is that reality is an undivided wholeness. In his book, *Wholeness and the Implicate Order*, he explains the theory that reality is an undivided wholeness by using the analogy of the hologram to describe the nature of reality. A hologram contains the information of the whole in each of its parts, and any part reflects the image of the whole. Bohm proposes that similarly reality is an unbroken wholeness in which each part contains the whole. His theory of quantum reality poses a hidden order that lies beneath the seeming chaos and lack of continuity of the individual particles described by quantum mechanics. Bohm names this hidden order or organizing principle the "implicate order"—the *source* of all visible matter, all manifestation on the material plane. He names the visible manifestation the "explicate order." The "holomovement" is the ground of all that is manifest, containing both the implicate and explicate order. The term "holomovement" describes the plenum out of which all forms of the material universe flow in the enfolding and unfolding process.

Bohm later adds to his theory the "superimplicate order," which is the source beyond all, transcending all. In Bohm's words: "This higher order is not basically the order of space and time, but the order of space and time unfolds from it and folds back into it …"[47] Bohm believed it is possible to "know" or to make "connection" with this "source of all." The process he envisions is evolutionary in nature and directed by consciousness. Bohm stated in a conversation with Renee Weber, "In nonmanifest reality it's all interpenetrating, interconnected, one. So we say deep down, the consciousness of mankind is one."[48]

•   •   •

Connections and commonalities exist not only between the new discoveries and theories in physics, General Systems Theory and Chaos Science, but also with other disciplines we have reviewed. Both quantum physics and metaphysical mystic teachings see the world as holistic interrelated systems. Physicist Max Planck wrote the following:

> In modern mechanics … it is impossible to obtain an adequate version of the laws for which we are looking, unless the physical system is regarded as a whole. According to modern mechanics (field theory), each individual particle of the system, in a certain sense, at any one time, exists simultaneously in every part of the system.

There is an excellent description of the "wholeness" of creation in Ephesians, 4:4-6. "There is one body, and one Spirit, … one God and Father of all, who is above all, and through all, and in you all." We also recall from Buddhist teaching that "When the oneness of the totality of things is not recognized, then ignorance as well as particularization arises, and all phases of the defiled mind are thus developed."

The following quotation from the writings of the the Christian mystic Nicolas of Cusa sounds very similar to David Bohm's theory of the folding and unfolding between the implicate and explicate order, the total of which he calls the "holomovement." "Divinity is the enfolding and unfolding of everything that is," writes Cusa. "Divinity is in all things in such a way that all things are in divinity." Bohm also proposed that there is a "superimplicate order" which is the source beyond all, transcending all. It is interesting to note that in the Hindu text *The Upanishads*, Brahman is called "the source and end of all, the unmanifest source of all manifestation."

Charles Fillmore, co-founder with Myrtle Fillmore of the Unity School of Christianity, taught the following, which is also similar to the theory of David Bohm.

God is substance; but this does not mean matter, because matter is formed while God is the formless … It is that which is the basis of all form yet enters not into any form of finality. It is a state of absolute Suchness, of absolute Emptiness which is absolute fullness.

Carl Jung also proposed a theory akin to Bohm's. According to Jung, there is a ground from which all reality springs, which he called a pleroma—the potential from which the physical world arises, which at each point, no matter how small, contains the whole.

CHAPTER FIVE

MASCULINE/FEMININE:
A MATTER OF BALANCE

The masculine, differentiating approach to the world, to the nature of reality, and to the nature of the relationship between the human beings and the world has reached a point of crisis. Yet, we also see now … the potential for great transformation and healing, a coming to wholeness by the tremendous resurgence of the feminine archetype. [This is] visible in a whole different approach to life—our scientific theories of the human psyche, the new sensibility of how human beings relate to nature and other forms of life on the planet—all of these reflect the emergence of the feminine archetype … which is manifesting a new sense of connection with the whole. This ideally could result in the … coming together of the masculine and feminine on many levels: between the human being and nature, between intellect and soul, between men and women.

Richard Tarnas, Ph.D.,
Historian and Professor of Philosophy

Sri Aurobindo, one of the greatest spiritual leaders and thinkers of the 20th century, describes the condition of our world in the following way:

> At present, mankind is undergoing an evolutionary crisis in which is concealed a choice of its destiny, for a stage has been reached in which the human mind has achieved in certain directions an enormous development, while in others, it stands arrested and bewildered and can no longer find its way.

Aurobindo does not leave us hanging over the abyss. He finds hope for humankind in "A life of unity, mutuality and harmony born of a deeper and wider truth of our being."[49]

An understanding of the "wider truth of our being" includes our realization of the duality of our nature—the masculine and feminine aspects that reside within each of us. Psychiatrist Roberto Assagioli, who developed the transpersonal therapy of psychosynthesis, cautions us to understand this duality. He writes, "We need to recognize that both masculine and feminine principles exist in their own rights, and that they are present—although in unique forms and different proportions—in every man and every woman."[50] As we all know, throughout history there has been a decided emphasis on valuing of the masculine principle, and devaluing of the feminine aspects of our nature. The feminine is often seen as being in a way "the frosting on the cake"—tasty but not necessarily needed. Aurobindo puts it in much more dramatic terms.

> A long tragic imbalance of the masculine has brought humankind to the moment when unless it recovers the feminine powers of the psyche—of intuition, patience, reverence for nature, knowledge of the holy unity of things, and marries these powers with the masculine energies of will, reason, passion or order and control, life will end on the planet. This marriage of the masculine with the feminine has to

take place in all of our hearts and minds, whether we are male or female.[51]

According to Riane Eisler it was the questions that haunt us all which led her to the studies that culminated in her remarkable book, The *Chalice and the Blade*. "Why do we hunt and persecute each other? Why is our world so full of man's infamous inhumanity to man, and to woman? What is it that chronically tilts us toward cruelty rather than kindness, toward war rather than peace, toward destruction rather than actualization?" These questions, claims Eisler, led her to a re-examination of our past, present and future, which took into account "the whole of human history" (including our prehistory as well as the whole of humanity—both its female and male halves). *The Chalice and the Blade* gives new insights into our cultural origins and attempts to persuade that neither war nor 'the war of the sexes' are divinely nor biologically ordained and that a better future is possible.

The human species emerged from the caves of the Paleolithic period, around 10,000 BCE in most areas. Men and women slowly developed more refined tools, pottery making, carpentry and weaving, while the development of agriculture and domestication of animals provided new food supplies. Although extremely primitive in early Neolithic times, new archeological findings show that many of these communities had stability and progressively more advanced growth over thousands of years. In Eisler's words, new archeological digs "reveal a long period of peace and prosperity when our social, technological and cultural evolution moved upward: many thousands of years when all the basic technologies on which civilization is built were developed in societies that were not male dominant, violent and hierarchic."[52]

Although long-held theory has claimed that male dominance was the result of the agrarian revolution, along with slavery and private property, there is new evidence to the contrary. Equality between the sexes in these ancient agrarian communities is verified by archeological evidence.

In these societies, the Goddess, or the feminine aspect of God, was worshiped as the giver and nurturer of all life, and nature was viewed with wonder and reverence. However, they were not, as many believed, matriarchies, but what Eisler calls "partnership" societies in which there was cooperation between the sexes. There were both priestesses and priests, and in later societies such as the Minoan, both queens and kings. There is evidence that these societies were quite egalitarian, with no underclass. Positions of authority functioned not for domination, but for service. No warrior class existed.

The rich information from archeological digs in ancient Neolithic sites across Europe and the Near East comes from the excavation of buildings and the retrieval and study of their contents, such as clothing, jewelry, food, furniture, containers, and tools. Burial sites are further abundant sources of information. Also the art, as in all civilizations, portrays the religious and social customs of the people. Anthropologist Paul Mellars believes that in the prehistoric periods, "art stands in many ways as the most impressive, enduring testimony."

As these artifacts were studied it was found that in these ancient Goddess-worshiping agrarian societies, tools were used primarily for production of useful objects; there were no heavy fortifications, no thrusting weapons, no caches of weapons. Research shows that their art did not include the idealization of armed might, cruelty, and violence-based power; there were no battle scenes or portrayals of heroic conquerors. Technology was used for the enhancement of life. Art depicted abundant symbols from nature, symbols associated with the Goddess as the giver and nurturer of life.

These ancient communities flourished in geographical locations that had either been fortuitously chosen or settled by fortunate happenstance. Fertile land, available water, pasture and sometimes abundant forests made possible heir growth and economic stability. Historian Marija Gimbutas writes in *The Gods and Goddesses of Old Europe* that "Old European locations were chosen for their beautiful settings, good water and soil, and availability of animal pastures ... but not for their defense values." In *Prehistoric Europe: From the Stone Age to the Early Greeks,* historian Phillip Van Doren Stern confirms that many villages were situated in "what would seem to us pleasant places, of mild weather with alternating rainy and dry seasons, of varied woodland, shrub and herbs, a land of hills and valley, of streams and springs, with alluvial reaches and rock shelters in cliffs."[53]

However, nomadic bands eking out a precarious living in harsher, colder, less fertile environs, were lurking in the background. There is evidence to suggest that by 7000 BCE, both in the Near East and in Old Europe there began a series of invasions that would last over many thousands of years. Two of the invading peoples were the Kurgans, who swept across prehistoric Europe in migratory waves, and the Semites, who came from the deserts of the south to invade Canaan. Both groups were warring peoples ruled by priests and warriors who brought with them male gods of war. Combined with natural disasters, this would eventually mean the demise, not only of the communities themselves, but of a whole way of life.

Accompanying this loss was the reduction of women and children to possessions of the male, changes in burial rites with "chieftain graves" accompanied by sacrificed wives and slaves, caches of weapons, and a general deterioration of the culture. Towns and villages disintegrated, magnificent painted pottery vanished as well as shrines, frescoes, sculptures, symbols and script. Whereas earlier European culture was peaceful and democratic with no indications of chiefs concentrating communities' wealth, all changed with the introduction of weapons and warfare.

Another confirmatory source of information about the Neolithic period comes from ancient myths and legends. *The World of Joseph Campbell,* volume I, tape II, "Transformations of Myths Through Time," portrays a vivid picture of the "city civilizations." During this era in these peaceful cities, where tools, not weapons, created wealth, where the people were "makers," not "takers," the Goddess was worshiped as the source of spiritual birth as well as the source of nature and the physical world. According to Campbell, "people lived in accord with nature and the rhythms of life." Although not quite utopian, for thousands of years, these communities survived peacefully and grew in complexity through many transformations.

Ancient poets wrote of times even more ancient. With perhaps the exaggeration that time lends a tale, the poet Hesiod writes of a "Golden Race" of the distant past that "all good things were theirs. The fruitful earth poured forth her fruits unbidden in boundless plenty. In graceful ease they kept their lands in good abundance, rich in flocks and dear to immortals." Hesiod goes on to tell of the invasion of lesser races of "silver," then "bronze." "In no way like the silver, dreadful and mighty, sprung from the shafts of ash," the "bronze" brought war. These people, Hesiod continues, "ate no grain, but hearts of flint were theirs, unyielding and unconquered."[54]

According to Eisler's research, a chronic theme of Mesopotamian legends is about times before the flood when people lived lives of plenty in an idyllic garden. The Goddess was often referred to as the Queen of Heaven. In fact, Biblical scholars connect these legends to parts of the Old Testament.

> Viewed in the light of the archaeological evidence … the story of the Garden of Eden is also clearly based on folk memories. The Garden is an allegorical description of the Neolithic, of when women and men first cultivated the soil, thus creating the first 'garden.' The story of Cain and Abel in part reflects the actual confrontation of a pastoral people, … and an agrarian people. Likewise, the Garden of Eden and

the Fall from paradise myths in part draw from historical events.[55]

In *The Chalice and the Blade*, Eisler takes exception to the long-held assumption that warfare, strife and poverty are simply the price we must pay for technological advance and the actuality of "human nature." The old argument that indeed "things have always been this way" is disproved by the new knowledge that on this earth have passed thousands of years of relatively peaceful progress, when the principles of both material and nonmaterial technologies were developed. The fundamental material technologies were flourishing, as well as increasingly sophisticated uses of natural resources such as wood fibers, leather, and later, metals in manufacturing. Research shows that nonmaterial technologies such as law, government, and religion likewise date back to Old Europe. Education, architecture, town planning and the arts thrived, as well as trade by both land and sea appeared. All of these were parts of what Eisler calls predominator or partnership societies.

One such partnership society that stayed intact the longest and which had the fullest and most remarkable development was the Minoan civilization on the island of Crete. A recent archeological excavation uncovered a highly developed civilization, amazing the scientific community. The development of Cretan civilization began around 6000 BCE, when immigrants arrived, probably from Anatolia. A seafaring people, they established primitive settlements along the coast. They brought agrarian technology and the veneration of the Goddess. They made steady technological and social progress over thousands of years, culminating in a civilization which thrived economically, socially and artistically.

The resulting city states which developed lived peacefully alongside each other. Neither the palaces or the cities themselves boasted military fortifications. Anthropologists have found that each King (or Queen) ruled his own domain in close harmony and peaceful coexistence with the others. Most early anthropologists took for granted that there were only male rulers; however, Leonard Cottrell, in his book *The Mystery of Minoan Civilization*, suggests that the evidence points more to a Queen as head of state, and recently more researchers have agreed. As portrayed by many frescoes, women were prominent in all aspects of life, including athletics, and were seemingly given "priority" in places of honor.

Although their lives were in many respects luxurious, there is no evidence of large caches of personal wealth amassed by the head of state or other administrative classes. General revenues were used to improve living conditions for all, and the evidence shows a remarkable feature of Cretan society—an equitable distribution of wealth.

Scholar Sir Leonard Wooley, has called Cretan art "the most inspired in the ancient world." It evidently exhibited a grace, joy, beauty, refinement and even whimsy that was unique. There was no trace in their art of destruction and oppression or of a dominating class. There were no scenes of the slaughter of battle or the hunt. Jacquette Hawkes writes in *Dawn of the Gods*, "Neither the depiction of a warrior monarch triumphing in the humiliation and slaughter of the enemy," nor manifestations of "pride and cruelty" were present in Cretan art.

In religion, the Goddess was supreme, as she had been for thousands of years in Neolithic society. Because of the veneration of the Goddess and the strong position of women in the Minoan society, it was thought to be a matriarchy by earlier anthropologists. More recently, that is thought not to be the case. Eisler describes the Minoan civilization as having developed a partnership or linking social model. Unfortunately, it was to be destroyed, as were the other similar societies before them, by natural disaster and invasions. According to Eisler, "In Crete, for the last time in recorded history, a spirit of harmony between women and men as joyful and equal participants in life appears to pervade."[56]

The Indo-European Achaeans seem to have been the first to seize power in Crete, and in the period of their ascendancy, known as the Mycenaean period, the changes were not so formidable. Not long after, barbarian warriors attacked, and by the eleventh century, this magnificent civilization had ended. The Goddess was now reduced to the consort of the male God, and slowly the feminine aspect of the divine nature was devalued, relegated into a usually very dim background.

Earlier in the Neolithic communities on the mainland of Europe and the Near East, as invasions of tribes such as the Kurgans and Semites progressed, there had begun to appear a decided difference in the art and artifacts of the people. Visual images of warrior gods replete with weapons became common. European prehistorian V. Gordon Childe traced the change from a peaceful and democratic culture as weapons and warfare were introduced. There is evidence that the Kurgans massacred most of the men and children after conquering an area, preserving the women as their concubines. Eisler points out that the Old Testament, Numbers 321:32-35, documents how the Semites treated the spoils of war. "Among the spoils of war taken by the invaders in their battle against the Midianites, there were, in this order, sheep, cattle, asses and thirty-two thousand girls who had no intercourse with a man."

The reduction of the status of women to all but a slave is everywhere in archeological evidence. "This glorification of the lethal power of the sharp blade accompanied a way of life in which the organized slaughter of other human beings, along with the destruction and looting of their property and subjugation and exploitation of their persons, appears to have been normal."[57]

It is interesting to note how the conditions during the late Neolithic, when this turnaround of the social order happened, fit the criteria laid out in chaos theory for dramatic change. Ongoing invasions from marauding hordes over centuries, combined with natural disasters, finally caused bifurcation points that brought massive disequilibrium into the social system. Society was ultimately reorganized into a different pattern from the "partnership" model to the "dominator" model.

Only by becoming aware of past human processes can humanity be sure to guide the world into a more positive future. Eisler puts it well.

> Now, thousands of years later, when we are nearing the possibility of a second social transformation—this time a shift from a dominator society to a more advanced version of a partnership society—we need to understand everything we can about this astonishing piece of our lost past. For at stake at this second evolutionary crossroads, when we possess the technologies of total destruction once attributed only to God, may be nothing less than the survival of our species.[58]

• • •

II. THE HISTORICAL FEMININE

In time, the teachings of all of the major religions have come to support a patriarchal philosophy. Even the teachings of Jesus, which exemplified both masculine and feminine values, were eventually subverted by the church hierarchy. Historians Will and Ariel Durant call the perversion of the teachings of Jesus a moral setback to the Christian world. In the name of Christianity, as well as other religions, terrible and cruel deeds have taken place. And throughout most modern history, women, one-half of humanity, have been deemed less worthy and even the bearers of sin to the world.

The qualities of the Goddess, or the feminine aspect of God, did not, entirely disappear. In Christianity, Mary the mother of Jesus, the Queen of Heaven, brought softness and compassion and accessibility, which reflected the words and teachings of Jesus more closely than the dictates of the Church Fathers. In the mystical tradition of Judaism, and rarely mentioned in Jewish education, the Shechinah is defined as the "female aspect of God or the presence of the infinite God in the world." She is also defined as "the luminous presence of the Divine, the great light who shines on all creatures."[59]

Religious beliefs underlie a culture's assumptions; other cultural aspects extrapolate those fundamental values. Recently researches have added the status of women to the equation as they have studied societies, with very interesting results. Historian G. Rattray Taylor, in *Sex in History*, has found that matrist periods (those when women and feminine values are accorded higher status) "are characteristically intervals of greater creativity, less social and sexual repression, more individualism and social reform."

Through his research, psychologist David Winter has come to the conclusion "that in systems terms male dominance is inextricably interrelated with the male violence of warfare." Also, "the re-idealization of male supremacy signals a shift toward the values and behaviors that historically fuel the violence of androcratic (dominator model) regressions." Theodore Roszak found "an underlying commonality among the men who at the turn of this century—and throughout history—plunged the world into war. This is the equation of masculinity with violence that is required if a system of force-based rankings is to be maintained." Psychologist David McClelland found "the 'softer' more 'feminine' values characteristic of the partnership model of society are part of a particular social and ideological configuration that stresses creation rather than destruction."[60]

The philosophy and policies of the conquering peoples during the late Neolithic and early historical periods have remained in place into the current era. At certain times and places we have seen a modification of these policies, times and places when research shows there was a rise in cultural and artistic achievement, as well as a more peaceful climate.

•   •   •

III. THE HISTORICAL MASCULINE

The power-based dominator political model of society is most powerfully and clearly expressed by Niccolo Machiavelli in his treatise *The Prince*, which gives advice to Lorenzo Di Piero de'Medici on the acquisition and maintenance of power. Machiavelli analyzes successful and unsuccessful uses of power to conquer and dominate politically and militarily, giving examples from antiquity to the then-current period of contemporary Italy. This "Machiavellian" classic has been considered the epitome of pragmatic advice to political heads of state and their entourage of leadership, the military establishments, as well as all those seeking political or military power. Studied and followed assiduously since that time (with some exceptions), *The Prince* remains an important part of the curriculum in political science departments of universities. Many current political and military leaders use it still.** The philosophy is called Realpolitic.

In *The Prince*, Machiavelli merely codifies practices in use for hundreds of years. As he documents the rise and fall of "princes," he condones murder, cruelty, destruction, dishonesty and any kind of intrigue that allowed a prince to establish power, and then suggests which particular method would be most effective in each situation.

Always geared toward the maintenance of power of the individual prince, Machiavelli advises that virtue has no value whatever unless it works to the above goal. "… the manner in which we live, and that in which we ought to live, are things … wide asunder … It is essential, therefore, for a Prince who desires to maintain his position to have learned how to be other than good and to use or not use his goodness as necessity requires ..."[61] He goes on to say in the most cynical way, "It is not essential that a Prince should have all the good qualities ... but it is most essential that he should seem to have them."[62] The welfare of mere people should not be a concern, according to Machiavelli, if it interfered in any way with the retention of power. Lives of countless civilians as well as soldiers could be sacrificed. He advised that men are "either to be treated kindly or utterly crushed, since they can revenge lighter injuries, but not graver."[63]

In another passage Machiavelli advises the Prince how to treat the people of a newly "acquired" state. "When a newly acquired state has been accustomed ... to live under its own laws and in freedom, there are three methods it may be held. The first is to destroy it; the second, to go and reside there in person; the third, to suffer it to live on under its own laws." However, he goes on to advise, "... there is no sure way of holding other than by destroying it ..." Not even people's minds were safe. "... matters should be so ordered that when men no longer believe of their own accord, they may be compelled to believe by force."[64]

Machiavelli saw war as the ultimate and only sure way of maintaining or acquiring power. "A Prince should have no care or thought but for war, and for the regulations and training it requires, and should apply himself exclusively to this as his peculiar province; for war is the sole art looked for in one who rules..."[65] In fact, Machiavelli writes, "... many are of the opinion that a wise Prince, when he has the occasion, ought dexterously to promote hostility to himself in certain quarters, in order that his greatness may be enhanced by crushing it."[66]

Has this philosophy really made its way into the 20th and 21st century western political and military strategies? Machiavellian ideas were clearly visible in German and Italian tactics in WWII, and discernible in various strategies used in Vietnam. Sadam Hussein in Iraq is surely as depraved as any Italian Price, as were the policies of destruction, rape and ethnic cleansing in Bosnia Herzegovina and Kosovo, Yugoslavia.

What strikes one in looking at history is that the Machiavellian philosophy—the sanctioning of warlike societies—has never worked. In the short term, there have been many ascendencies of men and states, but in the long run they fall again; none prevail. There is more than truth in the saying that "those who live by the sword, die by the sword."

As with any world view that is in place over time, the mores of the Dominator social model have been pervasive not only in the practice of political science, but in all aspects of life, including economics—the social science concerned with the production, distribution and consumption of wealth. Capitalism, perhaps the most productive economic system in history, has also been affected by dominator philosophy in the form of Social Darwinism.

In the mid-nineteenth century, Charles Darwin returned from his journey as official naturalist on the Beagle with a new theory of evolution that would shake the world. He published the results of his explorations, observations and investigations under the title *Origin of the Species*, and this theory was soon to be known as "Darwinism." Although others had speculated on and put forth similar ideas, Darwin (along with Alfred Russell Wallace) was the first to systematize them in a scientific way. Basic to Darwin's theory is the concept of the survival of the fittest: natural selection takes place over time by virtue of those qualities that best allow a species to survive.

Although Darwinism understandably had a tremendous impact on the conservative religious community, it also had an effect on economic theory and practice. With an hierarchical, power-based, "might-makes-right" belief system permeating the consciousness of most of humanity for so long, it is not surprising that "survival of the fittest" was interpreted by many to mean survival of the strongest, most powerful of the species over the weaker, and therefore the domination of the most powerful over the lower, less powerful, social classes. The implication of this theory, called Social Darwinism, was that humans live in a 'social jungle,' and the "fittest are those who can bring to the struggle superior force, superior cunning and superior ruthlessness."[67]

Social Darwinism became an apology for laissez-faire economics, and according to Howard L. Kaye in *The Social Meaning of Modern Biology*, the use of Darwinism became "an ideological buttress for competitive capitalism," as it sanctioned cruel economic social policies.[68] However, the economic interpretation of Darwin's theory by Social Darwinists was an erroneous one with which even Darwin disagreed. Kaye also points out that, although in Darwin's system natural selection played an important role in early human history, "the qualities selected were less those of physical strength and fecundity than those of intellect, sympathy, mutual aid, and more sense." Darwin felt that human beings had advanced more through "habit, the reasoning powers, instruction and religion."[69]

Although Social Darwinism prevailed through much of the nineteenth century, it has been challenged from its inception by those who questioned not only its validity, but its morality. As its most egregious consequences grew during the beginnings of the industrial revolution, less cutthroat economic policies were demanded by the people and their respective governments. However, it has reappeared in many other guises, one of the latest being "trickle-down" economics. Economist George Gilder, an advocate of this policy, claimed in his book *Wealth and Poverty* that the male's superior aggression was in itself of great social and economic value.

According to physicist Frizjof Capra in *The Turning Point*, "Promotion of competitive behavior over cooperation is one of the principle manifestations of the self-assertive tendency in our society. It is rooted in the erroneous view of nature held by the social Darwinists of the 19th century ..."[70] Not only did this theory have cruel consequences for many people during its ascendancy, but it has had disastrous consequences for our planet. With competition seen as the driving force of the economy, according to Capra, "the aggressive approach has become the ideal of the business world and this behavior has been combined with the exploitation of natural resources to create patterns of competitive consumption."[71] Although there are certainly responsible companies and corporations who practice capitalism in its highest form, all too often the consequences of thoughtless capitalism promoting wasteful production and consumption, along with the desire to minimize costs and thus maximize profits at any expense but theirs, has been depletion of our natural resources and pollution of our environment. The slogan that most captures this consciousness is "business is business," and thus, one supposes business is exempt from any moral standard that might be applied.

In keeping with this philosophy is the power that developed within the arms industry. The military-industrial complex is one of the better examples of an economic system gone awry, as power feeds power. Many historians believe that it is often the aggressive building up of military power of one nation and then another that ultimately leads to the onset of war. It is both telling and ironic that it was a five star general, Dwight D. Eisenhower, who warned the United States of this concentration of power, capable of perpetuating its existence beyond real need.

Although Darwinism has been established as the prevailing mode of evolution, new findings have modified the theory in interesting ways. As pointed out by many scientists, if survival was the only concern of the processes of nature, we would never have evolved beyond bacteria, which are perfectly adapted. Some scientists are now speculating that there is some sort of self-transcending drive inherent within evolution's own processes. This is very similar to the belief of Helena Blavatsky, the founder of the Theosophical

Society, who saw evolution "as an unfolding in progressive stages of inner or inherent potentialities, which exists within the process itself." Systems scientist Eric Jantsch has speculated that the work of biologist Lyn Margulis and chemist James Lovelock, formulators of the Gaia hypothesis, implies a cosmic scale of coevolution in nature. Biologist Barbara McClintock has found through her work that everything is one, and that there is no way in which a line can be drawn between things. Perhaps what we need is a new version of Social Darwinism, reflecting the changing consciousness of a world which is beginning to see the interconnectedness of all life, and universal cooperation as a feature of evolution.

• • •

IV. THE BOUNDARIES OF CURRENT SCIENCE

A great change is taking place in science regarding our understanding of the nature of reality. Revelations of quantum physics as well as what we are learning from general systems and chaos theory, dramatically sound the interrelationships of the masculine and feminine aspects of the living world. Whereas pre-quantum scientific materialism depicted the universe as objective—independent of any observer, and determined—predictable according to the laws of motion, we now know that the observer is bound intricately with the observation, and that the universe is fluid and unpredictable at its micro level. Subject and object, we find, are intimately related, and the intuition of the feminine principle is as fundamental as the objectivity of the masculine principle.

The science that has brought us this information has had remarkable success in bringing the world the technologies that have enhanced and lessened the burdens of life, and have extended life. Cultural historian Thomas Berry has concluded that "the scientific enterprise is the most sustained meditation ever carried out on the universe," and he compared what scientists have discovered to the revelations of the great religions. Teilhard de Chardin, both a scientist and priest, has called religion and science "the two conjugated faces or phases of one and the same complete act of knowledge." Many scientists today are working to make this a conscious realization. One of them is biochemist Linda Jean Shepherd, author of *Lifting the Veil: The Feminine Face of Science*. While recognizing the contributions of science, Dr. Shepherd also understands its shortcomings.

> Over the last fifty years, the magnificent achievements of science and technology have culminated in disastrous unforeseen consequences, tearing the very fabric of nature. The physics that landed a man on the moon also produced a world haunted by the threat of nuclear war. The chemistry that developed an incredible diversity of plastics also bequeaths a legacy of waste products that nature cannot reabsorb. The biology that brought forth the green revolution through fertilizers, herbicides and pesticides, threatens to yield a silent spring.[72]

"Caught up" by science since a child, Linda Shepherd was determined not only to pursue science, but to make a mark in her field. After receiving her doctorate, she determined to fit in the traditionally male profession of science. "In order to prove myself and succeed in the male realm of science," she writes, "I adopted the rational, analytical, hierarchical approach. I wanted to prove that I could be just as smart and competent as a man."[73]

Although successful both professionally and financially, she began to feel a sense of sterility in her job and yearned for work that would have significant meaning. Exploring these inner feelings, she came to understand that the element missing in much scientific work was the feminine principle to complement the masculine principle already at work. She came to believe "that the Feminine in each of us—the part of us that sees life in context, the interconnectedness of everything, and the consequences of our actions on future generations—can help heal the wounds of our planet."[74]

The empirical method of science initiated by Roger Bacon in the 16th century set the tone for subsequent practice, both in method and philosophy. The "scientific method," a product of Bacon and Newton, is in large responsible for what progress has been made. However, with our present knowledge that the planet is an interdependent ecosystem it is easy to see the flaws in Bacon's aspiration to inaugurate "the truly masculine birth of time." He declared that science must bind nature and all her children "to your service and make her your slave … to conquer and subdue her, to shake her to her foundations … to penetrate further … to storm and occupy her castles and strongholds, and extend the bounds of human empire."[75] We have indeed shaken Nature to her foundations and many scientists and ecologists are striving to prop her up again by finding ways to cooperate with, rather than subdue, our "mother."

To this end Linda Shepherd makes a great contribution as she points out the many ways that the practice of science may be enhanced by including the feminine approach to complement the masculine. When studying the qualities that are attributed to the Masculine versus Feminine Nature, it is easy to understand that either approach by itself could lead to disaster. The rational must be complemented with intuition, thinking with feeling, individual concerns with collective concerns, egalitarian structure with hierarchical, knowledge with compassion, efficiency with sensitivity.

The masculine vision, and thus the practice of science, has been objective, rational, logical and linear; qualities which, unbalanced, have led to a reductionist approach to the study of the natural world. Shepherd points out "While the power and the value of this approach cannot be denied, it neglects the relatedness of the parts. … When the masculine is used in conjunction with the feminine, the researcher can focus on the individual parts while simultaneously considering their relationship to each other and the environment."[76]

According to her observations, Shepherd finds that more often men emphasize separation and autonomy in their work and in their relations with other scientists. There is also a sense of competition between individual scientists in the various fields, which often slows progress on scientific endeavors that could benefit from better cooperation among researchers. Because of the immediate payoff expectation, many scientists are concerned with short term results.*** Although in the short term there have been payoffs in technology, in the long term these payoffs have at times been more destructive than helpful. Shepherd finds that "Science seems to promote a technological imperative like manifest destiny. We rarely consider the values built into a new technology, or how applications of science change the social pattern and the daily lives of people."[77] The masculine qualities of action and accomplishment are absolutely vital; however, when they are combined with the feminine qualities of reflection and relationship, untoward consequences may be avoided. Shepherd argues:

> We are just now realizing the hidden costs of the short-term approach to science and technology development—such as safe disposal of toxic chemical and nuclear wastes, soil depletion, and the squandering of natural resources. In looking for short term payoffs, we rarely consider the health and prosperity of future generations. Although the nurturing approach is fundamentally process-oriented, it is always with an eye to the long-term results and consequences.[78]

Shepherd believes that as "we experiment with new ways of combining thinking with feeling, aggression with receptivity, objectivity with subjectivity, multiplicity with hier-

archy, personal with professional, competition with cooperation, sensation with intuition, analytical reductionism with
relatedness ... beneficial unions will give birth to an entirely
new and wonderful science."[79]

In fact, the balance of the masculine and feminine principles in society, economics and science, as well as in all aspect
of our lives, could bring about an "entirely new and wonderful world."

*Please note that the researchers whom I have chosen to
quote here are mostly men. The feminine virtues have
never been erased in the male population, only devalued,
and therefore have gone unrewarded. It is greatly to their
credit that many men have resisted the powerful indoctri-
nation of society into the male dominator model.

**Of course there have been those who have disavowed this
philosophy. However, they have only rarely remained in
the mainstream of political and military events.

***There are many women scientists who fall in with the
established masculine patterns of doing science, as well as
many men who take a more cooperative and holistic
approach.

SECTION III:
FROM DEATH TO IMMORTALITY

The sheer volume of physical evidence for survival after death is so immense that to ignore it is like standing at the foot of Mount Everest and insisting that you cannot see a mountain.
Colin Wilson

Certainly our understanding of life is not complete without knowledge of our ultimate destination. Lacking that information, we have an incomplete "map of the territory." A map that cannot clearly direct and inform the choices we make in a seemingly unstable and turbulent world is of little use.

New studies have shown that what we humans believe, or as the case may be, disbelieve, has a profound effect upon our lives. People who have faith in something beyond themselves, often with an accompanying belief in an afterlife, tend to be healthier, live longer, and recover more easily from illness. Significantly, the majority of returnees from a near-death experience have a renewed commitment to life as well as a diminution of any fear of death. Most make different choices in their lives; many turn their lives completely around with a new assurance and understanding of what they are here to contribute.

However, we need not have a near-death experience, nor flounder blindly in seas of confusion, to become aware of the destination of the human spirit. The evidence is all around us, and ultimately, we can look within to find the verification in our own souls. As we become aware of our ultimate spiritual future, our present lives will take on added meaning and be even more precious as they give us the opportunity to grow in love and service toward an end that we will consider profound and worthwhile.

CHAPTER SIX

A MATTER OF LIFE AND DEATH

Physical birth is not a beginning; it is a continuing.
Everything that continues has already been born.
The Course in Miracles

It is no longer considered naive by many of "scientific
disposition" to believe in survival of human consciousness
after death. There has always been great argument in favor of
survival. However, beginning in the 19th century and continuing up to recent years the lay community, especially those
highly-educated, has been somewhat intimidated by Scientific Realism and the mechanistic-reductionistic approach of
modern science. New revelations in science, along with dis-
belief in the traditional view of an afterlife divided between a
heaven, where souls spring wings and play harps, and a hell,
where souls are subject to everlasting torment, led many to
give up any belief in survival after death.

The work of Descartes, Newton and others became the
basis for a scientific approach that produced excellent results
in the material or "macro" world, becoming the basis for a
world view or paradigm that held sway until the quantum
revolution that has challenged its most precious precepts.
Along with the revelation that the "mechanistic" world of

Newtonian physics—a world made of up discrete and predictable parts—was no longer valid, came the discovery that reality actually acts more like a quantum soup defined by relationships than by objective material properties.

Although there are hard core "realists" in the scientific community who do not admit the possibility of anything existing, or worthy to be studied, that one cannot see, hear, feel, taste, smell or touch, many in the scientific world, including Nobel Prize winners, are actually leading the advance toward the emergence of a different scientific approach to the study of reality, and therefore to a new paradigm or a fresh way of understanding the world.

Along with these changes has come the accumulation of powerful evidence for after-death survival of personal consciousness. Much of this evidence has been available for many years. Recently, with the new freedom to explore territories previously discouraged by the pervading scientific mind-set, studies have been undertaken which examine evidence, some new and some that has long existed, subjecting it to stringent investigation. People are beginning to feel free to share their own experiences without being ridiculed, and with increasingly open communication, the accumulation of evidence is mounting.

It is significant that all major religions and spiritual traditions have embraced the belief in a life beyond death. As author/mystic John White explains in *A Practical Guide to Death and Dying*, "Some see consciousness continuing in personal forms; some see consciousness reuniting with a cosmic intelligence or universal soul. And some see both happening through a continued process of spiritual evolution."

"The foundation of these traditions," White goes on to say, "is the mystical experience ... an experience in which knowledge of our cosmic origin and destiny is obtained directly through insight or revelation ... Mystical "knowing" is less susceptible than other evidence to scientific study, but is supported not only by the great religious prophets, but by untold numbers of revelations reported throughout history, often by our most revered and intellectually and spiritually gifted men and women. One of the truths revealed during the continuum of mystical enlightenment and an aspect of the perennial philosophy is that life is not only continuous, but ever evolving.

The grounds for belief in survival, however, issue from many other sources as well. The evidence for reincarnation is persuasive, though not completely indisputable. The Out of Body Experience (OBE) has been reported since antiquity, with the numbers of those experiencing it growing exponentially. The Near Death Experience (NDE), also in the literature for thousands of years, is being reported at an ever-increasing rate. When studied carefully, the most telling details are very hard to dispute. After Death Communications (ADC) are being reported apace, and again there have been innumerable instances reported throughout history. Although the scientists who study these phenomena are quick to say publicly that what they discover does not definitively prove survival, privately, they will say they are convinced that we experience an afterlife.

The evidence from all of these phenomena taken together makes a formidable case for survival. To reach any other conclusion after closely examining the evidence would require a very circuitous route in the reasoning process. The following will very briefly explore the pertinent facets of each phenomena.*

• • •

I. REINCARNATION

The doctrine of reincarnation, the belief that the soul returns to earth life in a new human body to continue its evolution, and its partner concept of karma, the law of cause and consequence, have been historically widespread through time and locale.** Karma does not concern itself with retribution; it is the means of achieving correction, balance and progress through the physical world.

The concepts of reincarnation and karma are fundamental to Hinduism, Buddhism, Jainism, Sikhism, and Zoroastrianism. In ancient Greece, reincarnation was a part of the metaphysical philosophy of the Pythagoreans, the Orphics and the Platonists. According to Stanislav Grof in his article "Survival of Consciousness after Death: Myth and Science," similar ideas can be found not only among various African tribes, American Indians, pre-Columbian cultures, the Polynesian Kahunas, the Gauls and the Druids, but were "also adopted by the Essenes, the Pharisees, the Karaites, other Jewish and semi-Jewish groups, and formed an important part of the kabbalistic theology of medieval Jewry."[81] The belief in reincarnation was also accepted by many early Christians. Origen, one of the great church fathers in the third century, taught that certain passages in the Bible could only be explained by the concept of reincarnation. However, this teaching was condemned and made heretical by the Second Council of Constantinople in 553 AD, at the command of Emperor Justinian. In modern times, more people believe in the theory of reincarnation than any other afterlife concept.

The evidence for reincarnation varies from mere intimations to empirical evidence difficult to dismiss: the feeling of déjà vu, having previously seen or experienced a certain scene or turn of events; the unexplainable attraction or repulsion immediate upon meeting certain people in one's life; interests and skills, strong tendencies and talents in areas not predictable from the context of one's life and one's genetic makeup; the full-fledged child prodigy, who at an early age exhibits profound ability far beyond any rational explanation.

Even more thought-provoking are the actual memories of a previous life, some spontaneous, and some uncovered by hypnotism and psychotherapy. From revelations of past lives can be found corroborative testimony very difficult to dismiss as coincidental or imaginary.

Spontaneous memories do occur, usually in response to some outside stimulus serving as a catalyst. The literature abounds with such examples; here follows one from a friend's experience. This gentleman was a prominent sculptor in the south. During a trip to Paris with his wife, also an artist, they were spending a day touring art galleries. At a small gallery, upon looking at a particular painting, nothing more striking than a pleasant landscape, my friend felt the immediate certainty that he had painted it. A flood of memories ensued, including detailed facts of the painter's life and how he had died. Upon checking these memories in an historical register at the library, he found that they were all true. (Of course, it is possible that he somehow received this information tele- pathically, but for what purpose? Unsought psychic informa- tion usually has a self-evident purpose.)

Past lives can also be remembered while the subject is under hypnosis. Two researchers stand out as among the most well known and respected in the field: Psychologist Dr. Helen Wambach, who researches cases revealed under hyp- nosis, and Dr. Ian Stevenson, a psychiatrist heading the divi- sion of parapsychology at the University of Virginia School of Medicine, who deals with spontaneous memory cases, mostly in children.

Dr. Wambach's book, *Reliving Past Lives: The Evidence Under Hypnosis*, has been praised for the scientific method- ology she devised for studying 1000 subjects who revealed past lives. These hypnotic sessions provided insights into past cultures, environments, and technology, as well as details about the personal lives of the subjects. The remem- bered events and details, as well as the cultural and economic information that was revealed in these session, when tallied with historical data, proved remarkably accurate. The majority of the subjects reported living humble, difficult, unromantic lives. According to Wambach:

The great majority of my subjects went through their lives wearing rough homespun garments, living in crude huts, eating bland cereal grain with their fingers from wooden bowls. Some of these lives were spent as primitive food-gatherers or nomadic hunters. But the majority of lower-class lives in all periods belonged to people who farmed the land ... If they were fantasizing these past lives, why would they choose such drudgery to recall?[82]

In her second book, *Life Before Life*, Wambach relates many case histories from her research. Case after case exhibit remembered details and documented situations that admit of no better explanation than reincarnation.

Dr. Ian Stevenson of the University of Virginia has spent over 30 years in the scientific study of reincarnation gathering over 3000 cases. His book, *Twenty Cases Suggestive of Reincarnation*, documents some of those he felt are most susceptible to scientific explanation. Most of his subjects have been children who claim to remember such facts as their former name, the area where they were born and its features, names and personal details of former relatives as well as details of their own past lives. The remembered facts check out amazingly well, even when a child's statement about his or her previous life was written down (usually by one of Stevenson's staff) before the former family could be reached and the statements verified.

Stevenson believes that some of his strongest most compelling evidence comes from birthmarks and birth defects corresponding to wounds that the person or child remembers occurring in the previous life, and which have been verified as having been inflicted on the previous personality. In *Noetic Sciences Review*, Winter, 1996, Keith Thompson reports the following from an interview with Stevenson. "In 43 of the 49 cases where we located [birth defects or birthmarks], medical documents confirmed the correspondence of the past wounds and the birthmarks on the living person."[83]

Stevenson has since published other books: *Children Who Remember Previous Lives: A Question of Reincarnation*, and *Where Reincarnation and Biology Intersect: A Synopsis.* His research is highly respected in the scientific community, and he, like most scientists, is guarded about claiming any *final* proof of reincarnation. However, he has argued that an impressive body of evidence exists and that nothing else explains it better. No alternative theory meets the test of proof.

Another source of accounts of remembered past lives comes from the process of psychotherapy. Stanislov Grof, a psychiatrist who has spent his career studying non-ordinary states of consciousness, states, "Past incarnation phenomena are extremely common in deep experiential psychotherapy and have great therapeutic potential. … A therapist who does not allow experiences of this kind to develop in his or her clients or discourages them when they are spontaneously happening is giving up a powerful mechanism of healing and personality transformation."[84] Memories of past lives can also elucidate the workings of karma, providing a means to release destructive karmic ties. "Karmic experiences," Grof explains, "are clearly connected with various emotional, psychosomatic, and interpersonal problems of the individual. … In some instances, they underlie immediately and directly psychopathological symptoms. … These experiences thus provide not only an understanding of psychopathology, but also one of the most effective therapeutic mechanisms."[85] Grof has observed that by reliving past life experiences, people can come to an understanding of the human dynamics involved, and experience a cleansing of past karmic bonds, leading to a feeling of liberation and even bliss. In his book *The Human Encounter With Death*, Grof documents many cases when this transformation has taken place.

When examining the full profusion of evidence that

supports a belief in reincarnation, one cannot but agree with Ian Stevenson that nothing else explains it better. Philosophically, combined with the concept of karma, reincarnation answers many questions about life itself. We all observe obvious unfairness in the world which, in the bounds of one lifetime, suggests a seemingly unjust universe. Most of us also realize that we are not going to "graduate" from the school of life without more semesters.

Furthermore, the concept of reincarnation fits with a new theory of evolution now emerging from scientific data—that of an ever-evolving universe moving toward a supreme culmination. James S. Perkins writes in *Experiencing Reincarnation*, "Clearly, reincarnation and karma are the changeless laws, by means of which Man accomplishes his spiritual evolution. ... The cyclic movement spirals upward, the rhythmic growth is an unleashing of hidden potentials ever unfolding toward perfection. The growth of the Soul is directed to attainment of the fullness of the stature of divinity that has been existent from the beginning."[86]

• • •

II. THE OUT-OF-BODY EXPERIENCE

The term "out of body experience" (OBE) is self-defining, referring to maintaining normal consciousness while at the same time experiencing yourself out of, or away from your body. Most often the physical body is then seen from a distance by the departed consciousness. This "consciousness" can move around, sometimes even travel great distances, and is often aware of being in a body of finer etheric material. Older terms for this experience, astral projection and astral travel, are prominent in much esoteric literature and have been reported since antiquity.

The projection of the etheric body from the physical body can be spontaneous or induced. An OBE is often experienced as part of the "after death experience," which can occur in the wake of a physical crisis: an accident, during a medical operation, in the course of severe life threatening illness. It can also happen spontaneously for no apparent reason, occasionally while in deep meditation, or to escape an intolerable situation. A psychiatrist friend of mine told me of a patient, a young boy, who repeatedly told him of the travels he took while his body was confined to an iron lung. Unfortunately, my friend did not believe him.

With the proper direction and concentration, many people who have experienced this phenomena spontaneously have been able to develop the ability to leave the body at will. There have been many accounts through the years of yogis and spiritual adepts who have mastered astral projection and astral travel. Paramahansa Yogananda, the founder of The Self-Realization Fellowship in the United States, relates his experience of astral travel in his classic book *Autobiography of a Yogi*.

As a young man of twelve, Yogananda had been commissioned by his father to deliver a letter to a friend in Banares. However, since his father no longer knew his friend's address, it was to be provided by a mutual friend, Swami Pranabnanda. When Yogananda arrived at his home, the Swami not only did not need to read the letter of introduction provided by Yogananda's father, but after closing his eyes in meditation for a few minutes, he announced to Yogananda that Nath Babu, his father's friend, would arrive in thirty minutes. To Yogananda's great puzzlement, in thirty minutes Nath Babu did arrive with a strange story. Thirty minutes ago, said Nath Babu, Swami Pranabnanda had approached him by the Ganges and told him that Yogananada was waiting for him at the Swami's home and would he please come there. Swami Pranabnanda, however, had never left Yogananda's presence.

Many cases of OBE's are associated with the experience of dying and nearly dying. Elizabeth Kubler-Ross reports hundreds of cases from her work with the dying when patients have shared accounts of OBE's that happened prior to actual death. She became convinced that death is simply a transition to a different state of consciousness. The literature is also rich with accounts of OBE's that have no connection with physical trauma or dying. Psychologist Dr. Robert Crookall has investigated and analyzed thousands of cases of all types of OBE's and reported his findings in seven books. British parapsychologist Celia Green has studied and analyzed approximately 400 cases of OBE's which she has documented in her book *Out of the Body Experiences*. D. Scott Rago has edited a book, *Mind Beyond the Body*, composed of fifteen articles reviewing the best of the studies made on the subject of OBE's. These volumes represent but a small part of the work done in this field, altogether offering impressive testimony that this is a valid category of human experience.

It is a legitimate question to ask what form, if any, the human consciousness takes upon leaving the body. There are reports of personal, conscious, out-of-body awareness both within a defining form and without a defining form. (Sometimes this appearance is described as a "light" or "energy" body.) However, it is interesting to note that experience without defining form is usually reported from a very high state of consciousness when the entity is aware of being a part of all there is—a true cosmic consciousness. With this taken into consideration, there is a great deal of accord within the esoteric literature, as well as in reports of OBE's, NDE's (near death experiences) and After Death Communications (ADC's), regarding the extra-physical form or body.

In ancient Greece, Pythagoras taught that mortals had, in addition to their physical body, a subtle or second body, which he called the "envelope of the soul, the instrument of the spirit." In fact, throughout the major religious traditions there have been reports from antiquity onward of the several layered sheaths of the human vehicle. Although the names for these have been many, in the current esoteric tradition it is generally agreed that there are four interpenetrating bodies that enclose the human soul: physical, astral, mental and causal. At death, or upon leaving the body in astral projection, the personal consciousness is then housed in the astral body. In the case of a death, one remains in the astral body until such time, sooner or later, when the soul moves on toward the mental and then causal planes. We are all aware of matter and even music moving at such a high frequency that we can neither see nor hear it. In the same manner, each body sheath is made respectively of finer or more subtle material, each progressively possessing a higher frequency, usually only able to be seen in the plane to which it corresponds.

Jan Price, founder with her husband John Price of the Quartus Foundation, a spiritual research and communications organization, is also a collaborator with him in writing many inspirational books. Recently she had a sudden heart attack during which she was transported to the realms of the afterlife. She relates her whole experience in *The Other Side of Death*. Of the appearances of herself and others on "the other side," she reports that, "The people I saw looked much like those from the physical world, though there was a glow about them. It's not that you get another body; it's more like you shed the one you've been wearing and another one you already have is revealed."[87]

In *The Light Beyond*, Raymond Moody related the descriptions of the body as observed by the NDEers included in his study.

> Most people say they are not just some spot of consciousness when this happens. They still seem to be in some kind of body even though they are out of their physical bodies. They say the spiritual body has shape and form … It has arms and a shape although most are at a loss to describe what it looks like. Some people describe it as a cloud of colors or an energy field.[88]

If during an NDE a person goes to an afterlife realm and either sees or meets with people or relatives, bodies are often experienced as having more substantial form. The happiest note is that bodies that were old, deformed, or crippled on leaving earth existence are now whole and in the prime of life.

• • •

III. THE NEAR DEATH EXPERIENCE

Due to new medical technology, more and more people are being brought back from the brink of death. Consequently NDE accounts are growing rapidly, as are the researchers committed to submitting them to scientific investigation. The "near death experience" not only has relevance for the question of survival itself, but for the nature of survival. Those who have experienced an NDE have brought back information about how and where we exist in the afterlife, how we are occupied and our relationships with others, and the questions of heaven, hell, purgatory and the nature of time.

The "near death experience," so termed by Dr. Raymond Moody in his ground-breaking book *Life After Life* is described by the subject, usually seriously ill or physically traumatized, as becoming aware of being conscious, although seemingly dead. There is a core experience that Moody has described and that has been verified by other researchers.

(1) There is a sense of being dead, (2) usually prompted by being separated from and viewing the body, often from above. (3) During this time, the person experiences profound peace and well-being, not only able to observe all that is going on around him but also able to accurately relate it at a later time. The experience sometimes ends here, with the person returning to the body. The next aspects are experienced often, but less frequently than the first three. (4) At this point, if the person has not yet returned to the body, he or she usually enters a dark tunnel and travels at breathtaking speed toward

an indescribably beautiful light, (5) where they are often met by friends or relatives who are described as glowing or bathed in light and/or (6) are met by a radiant being of light who guides them through (7) a life review. (8) Some NDEers are guided or travel to various places in this dimension where they see Cities of Light and/or Temples of Learning. (9) At this point or possibly before, the being of light either informs the person that he or she must return or gives them a choice to do so or not. Usually reluctantly, from a sense of obligation, they agree to return.

There are many variations of this scenario and not every person experiences the same events nor interprets them in the same way. Nevertheless these aspects are common to all NDEers in some degree, with the deeper experiences usually including most of them. Also, the language that these people grope for to explain and describe experiences outside the common understanding is unusually similar.

It is fascinating that there is so much agreement between those who have reported what they have observed or learned about the after-life dimension from experiencing an OBE, NDE or having had an After Death Communication. The information they provide not only appears to validate much that has been taught in "the ancient wisdom," often called the perennial philosophy, but is also in accord with relevant scientific data. As we know from our studies of science, all matter, from the total universe to the smallest atom, is in perpetual motion. The differences in forms, both in density and clarity, are determined by the frequency of the motion— whether higher or lower. Consciousness itself has a frequency level, and, as reported by many "returnees," produces form at its own frequency. This suggestion gives credence to the old adage that we are what we think.

It has long been believed in esoteric wisdom that what we are and the substance of our thoughts—our consciousness— carries a vibration that impresses the energy field around us. Patterns, conditions and situations called forth by the level of our consciousness are then externalized in our lives. John Price wrote in *The Planetary Commission* that "everything comes to you or is repelled from you based on the vibration of your energy field, and the vibration is established by your belief and convictions."

Jan Price explains, "Structure and environment continue to be brought into expression as a reflection of consciousness—as mind energy coming into form and experience—but the manifestation [in the after-life dimension due to its higher frequency] is so much faster."[89] Famous psychic Betty White, whose communications with her husband from the afterworld are reported in *The Unobstructed Universe*, has called the frequency of the individual consciousness a "sort of magnetic energy field."

It seems apparent from the evidence that each person coming to the astral world after death awakens in the conditions—mental, physical and spiritual—that he or she has created for him or herself in the life just completed. During her NDE, Jan Price found herself in a beautiful environment with flowers, trees, people, and even dogs and other animals—all having substantial appearance. She also traveled to other more rarefied planes and saw gleaming cities of light and temples of learning. One she described as a "structure of supernal beauty. It was vast, of the purest white, ... paths led to the structure from all directions, with many people coming and going."[90]

A research subject named Daryl, who had an NDE as a result of being electrocuted, described in Kenneth Ring's book *Life at Death* that while traveling toward brilliant lights, "I moved closer to the lights and realized they were cities built of light." He described cathedral-like temples rearing around a center of gold and silver light. Entering a building of light, he found that "this cathedral was literally built of knowledge. This was a place of learning ..." Stella, another research subject of Ring, said, "There was this tremendous burst of light and, I was turned ... to the light. I saw at a great distance a city. And then I began to realize that the light was coming from within this city ...."[91]

Other travelers in this realm, however, have reported darker and more depressing conditions. Dr. George Ritchie, in *Return from Tomorrow*, an account of his own very deep and profound experience, describes one of the scenes he encountered. "The plain was crowded, even jammed with hordes of ghostly discarnate beings; nowhere was there a solid, light-surrounded person to be seen ... And they were the most frustrated, the angriest, the most completely miserable beings I had ever laid eyes on."[92]

Emmanuel Swedenborg, the renowned philosopher, who according to his writings was privileged to spend much time in the after-life domain, paints a similar scene in the following passage. "A man who is of [evil or immoral] character comes after death into a society hell similar to himself. And then in every particular respect, he acts in unison with it; for he thus enters into his own form, that is, into the states of his own mind."[93]

It turns out that there is no heaven, hell or purgatory where one is sent by judgment of a deity. Each of us rises or falls to the planes of existence that are of our own, chosen frequency, which often *seem* like heaven, hell or purgatory. P. M. H. Atwater, puzzled by the strangeness of her own three NDE's, researched the subject and reported her findings in *Coming Back to Life*. She speaks of the frequency levels with this analogy: "You fit your particular spot on the dial by your speed of vibration."[94] As C. W. Leadbeater, the great metaphysical teacher, writes in *Life After Death*, "There is no reward and punishment from outside, but only the actual result of what the man himself has done and said and thought while here on earth. In fact, the man makes his bed during the earth life and afterwards has to lie on it."[95] It is reassuring to note that the vast majority of experiences reported from NDEers are positive, even blissful. This is underscored by the fact that most of those who have experienced the afterlife do not wish to return to their life on earth.

As with the interpenetrating body sheathes described earlier—the physical, astral, mental and causal—there are also reported planes of existence in the after-life dimension that correspond to them. Bill and Judy Guggenheim have found evidence through their work with "after death communications" for what they call levels of consciousness or levels of love. They report,

> Some people who have had a prolonged near-death experience or have explored the afterlife during a number of out-of-body journeys report that it is composed of an unlimited number of subtle gradations or levels. These apparently extend from the highest, brightest, celestial realms, which are filled with love and light, down through a midrange of grayer, darker levels, to the lowest worlds, which are virtually devoid of all light love, and emotional warmth.[96]

As we descend or rise to the level of our own consciousness, we are not consigned there forever. The moment one's consciousness turns upwards, wearing out baser desires and habits, to aspire toward the good, that person is immediately helped by those who stand ever-ready. From wherever one begins on the astral plane (according to many metaphysical teachings there are seven levels), there is continuous progression to higher planes, first from the astral to the mental and ultimately to the causal—the deep center of immortal consciousness. How quickly this happens depends on the aspiration of the individual soul.

Our relationships and occupations in the afterlife bear a similarity to what we know in earth life, with some major differences. There are no "physical" needs or desires to be fulfilled. Those who come to this dimension steeped in a culture of "getting and spending" and achieving status and power through material gain have a more difficult time adjusting. M. Scott Peck's novel, *In Heaven as on Earth*, portrays a vision of the afterlife. The main character, a well-known psychiatrist and author, discovers a community of those who have been so occupied in accumulating wealth, power and status through business and financial negotiations on earth, that they continue to live lives of intrigue and competition, trying to best each other in ephemeral gains that have no reality. To Peck, this is a type of hell. Although fiction, this projection of Peck's beliefs is reflected in many reports of returnees.

NDEers report meeting friends and loved ones. They find that people live together in communities of similar interests and are occupied generally with pursuits that enhance their growth and knowledge and/or are engaged in helping others in various ways. Ruth Montgomery writes in *The World Beyond*, "Our purpose here is the same as there, to do that which God wishes for each of us. No two of us are alike and our missions down through the ages have varied as much as the earthly personalities with which we drape our spirit."[97]

Shortly after Peck's main character arrives in the afterlife, he is asked to work helping others make adjustments to this new dimension. Later, he graduates to a higher plane where he joins a community of souls who are working with events on the earth's international scene to bring forth God's plan. The validity of such a scenario is confirmed by reports from many returnees. Wherever we are on the planes of consciousness, love is the ultimate virtue; as Swedenborg teaches, we gravitate to the places, people and occupations that reflect our highest love.

A very important part of the NDE, perhaps the most important, is the life review reported by so many returnees. Many studies have now been done of the after effects of the NDE, and, next to losing any fear of death, the effects of the life review are the most life changing and life enhancing. In *Heading Toward Omega*, Kenneth Ring deeply explores the life review phenomena that he claims "enables one to see or understand his entire life so that it is clear what truly matters in life."[98] A Being of Light, described variously as follows, is usually the catalyst for the life review.

A gentleman who nearly suffocated to death met "... a most beautiful being. It was neither a man nor a woman, but it was both. I have never, before or since, seen anything as beautiful, loving and perfectly pleasant as this being. An immense radiant love poured from it. An incredible light shone through every single pore of its face." Another NDEer included in Ring's research described a being of light with a glow that engulfed every corner of the room. "Even though the brightness was intense, you could still make out something of the features ... and form ... and the light also provided warmth and love."[99] Jan Price saw a "shimmering, iridescent light" begin to take on a shape. "A woman of breathtaking beauty appeared as I watched in awe," as she materialized "from pure light to visible, substantial form. ..."[100] Both Kenneth Ring and Raymond Moody believe, as do I, that the Being of Light is often, if not always, the manifestation of the person's Higher or Divine Self.*** Jan Price intuited this identification during her experience. "... I felt myself being absorbed. I was no longer just the entity I knew of as me, but more, so much more. The eyes I stared into were mine, the eyes of my soul."[101]

The following four experiences are reported by Kenneth Ring in *Heading Toward Omega*. One gentleman who suffered a heart attack while raking leaves had a similar life review experience. First, he relates "A brilliant white-yellow warm pillar of light confronted me ... and the greatest feeling of warmth and love and tenderness became part of me. ... Instantly, my entire life was laid bare and open to this wonderful presence ...." Without words, but with instant mental communication, he was asked "What had I done to benefit or advance the human race? At the same time all my life was presented instantly in front of me and I was shown or made to understand what counted." It was all done with absolute unconditional love and forgiveness.

As the result of an automobile accident, Janis experienced an NDE and a life review that illustrates the sense of time involved. She claims that in a split second "I saw my whole life pass right by me ... all chronological. All precise ... My whole life." Hank's account illustrates the altered awareness the experience can bring. "Everything I had ever known from the beginning of my life I immediately knew about ... I had total and complete, clear knowledge of everything that had happened in my life—even little minute things I had forgotten ... I realized that there are things that every person is sent to earth to realize and to learn ... To discover that the most important thing is human relationships and love and not materialistic things." Daryl was shown "what my life had done so far to affect other people's lives using the feeling of pure love that was surrounding me as the point of comparison. And I had done a terrible job ... using love as the point of comparison."[102]

An account from *Coming Back to Life* by Phyllis Atwater makes clear the new perspective about life derived from the near death experience. After her life review, she reflected,

> I had no idea, no idea at all, not even the slightest hint of an idea, that every thought, word and deed was remembered, accounted for and went out and had a life of its own once released; nor did I know that the energy of that life directly affected all it touched or came near. It's as if we must live in some kind of vast sea or soup of each other's energy residue and thought waves, and we are each held responsible for our contributions and the quality of "ingredients" we add.[103]

There is no external source of judgment during this experience—only unconditional love and forgiveness for any misdeed. The judgment comes from one's self. As one NDEer stated, "You are shown your life—and you do the judging. You have been forgiven all your sins, but are you able to forgive yourself for not doing the things you should have done?" According to all who have had this experience, you learn that human relationships are most important and giving love and understanding to others is the greatest accomplishment in life.

Also, in *Heading Toward Omega*, Kenneth Ring examines the meaning of the near-death experience in the actual lives of the returnees. His findings have been verified by many others. First, as we have mentioned, NDEers no longer have any fear of death. In fact, studies have shown that even those who have read or heard about an NDE have reduced anxiety about death. In the following, Ring sums up his findings about the long-term effects of an NDE.

> After NDE's, individuals tend to show greater appreciation of life and more concern and love for their fellow humans, while their interest in personal status and material possessions wanes. Most NDEers also state that they live afterward with a heightened sense of spiritual purpose and, in some cases, that they seek a deeper understanding of life's essential meaning. Furthermore, these self-reports tend to be corroborated by others in a position to observe the behavior of NDEers.[104]

There have been many alternative theories offered to explain the phenomena connected with the near-death experience. It has been suggested that these events could result from the effect of drugs, hallucinations, delusions, or mental illness in general. However, in some cases, drugs were never taken or administered. The experience of hallucinations and delusions are quite different from the core experience of the NDEer, and those who have had an NDE are reported to be better adjusted than ever before in their lives.

Neurological explanations, such as Cerebral Anoxia (insufficient oxygen to the brain) have also been suggested to explain the phenomena of the NDE. As Ring says in *Life at Death*,

> Any adequate neurological explanation would have to be capable of showing how the entire complex of phenomena associated with the core experience (that is, the out-of-body state, paranormal knowledge, the tunnel, the golden light, the voice or presence, the appearance of deceased relatives, beautiful vistas and so forth) would be expected to occur in subjectively authentic fashion as a consequence of specific neuro-logical events triggered by the approach of death.

It would not be difficult, Ring argues, to posit a number of causes for parts of the experiences, but since neurological explanations should be able to provide a comprehensive explanation of *all* aspects of the NDE, he believes "It is fair to conclude that physiological or neurological interpretations of near death experiences are so far inadequate and unaccept-able."[105]

•   •   •

IV. AFTER DEATH COMMUNICATIONS

The "after death communication" (ADC) is by far the most common experience of those we have discussed. In their book *Hello From Heaven*, Bill and Judy Guggenheim quote a report undertaken by the National Opinion Research Center and published in "American Health," which finds that "42% of Americans believe that they have been in contact with someone who has died. And 67% of widows believe they have had a similar experience." In their definition of an ADC, the Guggenheims do not include contacts made through intermediaries such as a psychic or medium. They define an ADC as a "spiritual experience that occurs when someone is contacted directly and spontaneously by a deceased family member or friend (who) initiates the contact by choosing when, where and how he or she will communicate." The Guggenheims have identified twelve types of ADC's.

Contacts are made with relatives and friends from the after-life dimension for several reasons, the most common is to give reassurance of their well-being. Many contacts are made to give warning of an impending harmful event, or in some way to give protection. Contact is sometimes made when a loved one is in great psychological distress, or contemplating suicide. In some cases, the deceased is trying to communicate information needed by a loved one, and in others wishes to effect the closure of some unfinished business.

The following are three examples from *Hello From Heaven* of ADC's of reassurance from a child to the parent. The first two are termed Auditory ADC's. At dawn, the parents of an eleven-year-old boy were returning from the hospital where their son had died of cancer. Just as the father looked toward the sunrise, he audibly heard his son's voice say "It's all right, Dad" and instantly he experienced a sense of profound peace. Carla, a school teacher in North Carolina lost her five year old daughter due to a brain tumor. Some months later, on her way to visit the grave she internally heard her daughter's voice say strongly, "Don't worry, Mom. I'm not there. I'm fine. I'm with Granpa and the other people who have died before me."

The next example is of a Full Appearance, Visual ADC. Anne lost both of her sons when the older boy tried to rescue the younger from drowning, and a year later she had the following experience: "All of a sudden, I felt there was someone in the room with me. When I turned, Bobby was standing there leaning on the refrigerator! He looked healthy and happy ... very solid and so real that it seemed I could have touched him … (His) eyes were glowing … He gave me the most wonderful smile." She felt he was telling her "we are both fine. We're all right. Just get on with things and be at peace with yourself."

Bill Guggenheim experienced an auditory ADC that saved the life of his child. One afternoon while in the front of his home, he heard a distinct but calm voice say "Go outside, check the swimming pool." He found his baby son floating straight up in the pool two inches below the water. The child was rescued in time with no unfortunate after-effects.

Pauline had contact with a deceased relative during an out-of-body experience, called an OBE ADC, during which she traveled with her recently murdered husband to the after-life realm. "We went through a tunnel … and there was a white light at the end … Art was perfectly healthy …" She learned that her husband, Art, was being cared for in a "halfway" house after the shock of the sudden violent death. Pauline further related "he was working with flowers. I've never seen such beautiful flowers … There were roses … and butterflies. It was all so pretty." She then proceeded to return through the tunnel and reenter her body.

Another fascinating category of this experience is called a Telephone ADC. In this case, the phone actually rings, and upon answering, you hear the voice of a deceased loved one. There is never a dial tone or a disconnect sound. Ellyn, who had lost her 12 year old daughter, Ashley, to leukemia, was very ill herself. One evening as Ellyn was preparing dinner, the telephone rang. Ashley's voice came over the line sounding strong and healthy. Ellyn said "Ashley, are you okay?" Ashley's voice answered, "Mommy, I'm okay. I just called to tell you that you're going to be okay too." Then the phone went dead with no dial tone or disconnect sound. Six months later, after lung surgery, Ellyn was making a full recovery.

Some seek to explain these experiences as hallucinations brought on by great grief. However, there are many recorded cases of those who receive an ADC before they know the communicator is dead. One such case happened with Darcie, who went to inform her mother's best friend, Rose, of her mother's death. Before she could tell the news the friend, Rose said, "the strangest thing just happened. Your mother came through the wall of my apartment and said, 'I have always loved you and I always will.' Then she left."[106] There are also cases when two people have experienced an ADC at the same time, able to act as witnesses for each other.

According to the Guggenheims, "an ADC experience is evidential when you learn something you did not know and had no way of knowing before. For instance, you may be told the location of an object that is lost and later confirm the accuracy of the guidance."[107] In the examples given in *Hello From Heaven*, people are guided to money, insurance policies and valuables that have been left behind in a secret place by the deceased. Loved ones have also been guided to fortuitous solutions of problems by the communication of needed information.

The insights gleaned from those who have experienced an ADC corroborate what is learned from the NDE. Like NDEers, many find a world of beauty, joy, love, harmony, and light. Everything is very much alive. The communities include magnificent cities and beautiful countrysides. There are flowers, plants and trees all with vibrant colors, birds sing and butterflies fill the air. And, as with NDEers, not all have the same experience. "It appears," explain the Guggenheims, "that our own thoughts, feelings and actions will determine the level of existence we will initially inhabit ... We will be neither rewarded nor punished ... Instead, we will ultimately go to the place we have rightfully earned according to the amount of love, compassion, and kindness that we have demonstrated during our life on earth."[108]

They also found spiritual progression is up to the individual, since we each have free will. We can choose to remain 'asleep' or 'awaken' to our own and others' spiritual reality. Much is accomplished through forgiveness and prayer, both for ourselves and others. One young woman returned to plead with her father to forgive and pray for her murderer, for the sake of them both. Our thoughts and our prayers are felt, they tell us, in the afterlife dimension as they are on earth.

The Guggenheims suggest that widespread belief in the reality of ADC's (as well as OBE's and NDE's) has the potential to change the world. They wonder how universal acknowledgment that we are all eternal spiritual beings would affect how we regard ourselves, others and life in general. "Such global awareness," they suggest, "could enhance our understanding and acceptance of one another, knowing we are all equal participants in the same sacred spiritual journey."[109]

James Redfield, author of *The Celestine Prophecy* and *The Tenth Insight* strongly agrees. He believes that the knowledge of an afterlife that continues the growth process, as well as an understanding of the purpose of the life review and the birth vision, would change the way we see ourselves and our relationship to the world. He writes, "When we are able to remember what all of humanity is supposed to do, starting right now, from this moment, we can heal the world."[110]

*The discussion included in this text that deals with the evidence for survival only touches the surface of the many available resources. The reader is referred to the references in the bibliography that not only give abundant examples, but deal with the possible alternative explanations that are often given for NDE'S and ADC'S.

**Reincarnation includes only the belief of return of the human to another human body. Transmigration is the belief that souls can return in an animal body.

***The Being of Light is at times interpreted to be a religious figure, occasionally Jesus, and sometimes God.

****The following books have in-depth discussions of the various alternative causes suggested for the NDE. *Life at Death* by Kenneth Ring, Ph.D., and *The Light Beyond*, by Raymond A. Moody, Jr., MD.

SECTION IV:
FROM CHAOS TO BEAUTY

Dramatically illustrated by the fact that the flutter of a butterfly's wings can effect a hurricane across a continent, it has been demonstrated by quantum physics and chaos science that the part and the whole are so intimately connected that the smallest change in one effects the other. In the same way, we humans are never able to do just one thing. All of our choices in words and deeds and even thoughts impact not only our own lives and those closest to us, but the entire planet as well. As expressed in *The Course in Miracles*, "There are no idle thoughts. All thinking produces form at some level." It is daunting to know that all we find wrong with our world is of our own doing. The good news is that we can do it differently. With the realization that every choice we make reverberates throughout our planet, we can take hold of our future. This gives us a new vision of human nature and the possibilities for change.

Fortunately, recent research, supported by ancient philosophy, has found that the consciousness of a critical mass of human beings, enlightened with awareness of the true nature of their humanity and with dedication and energy can, through their thoughts and actions, redirect our future from chaos to beauty. Since we are all connected, the force of this elevated consciousness will become manifest by more and more individuals until the new world view becomes established wisdom.

The following chapters illustrate how humanity is beginning to make new choices in areas of particular social concern, such as health care and economics. They also document how groups of people are choosing to live and act for the good of all, acting out the unity that is our true reality.

CHAPTER SEVEN

HEALTH AND THE HEALING ARTS

"The real cure is the realization that at the most essential level, we are all 'untouchables'—utterly beyond the ravages of disease and death."
Larry Dossey, MD

When a world-view begins to change, the reverberations are felt through all systems of a society. As physics, chaos science and general systems theory began to paint a new view of the world—a world that is fluid and in process which can only be understood holistically, our idea of the human body and its interactions within itself and with the environment began to change as well. As our "map of the territory" has expanded, so have our choices in health care.

Health and healing are issues of vital importance to every family as well as every individual. More often than not, in the past, most people have not questioned the wisdom of their physicians or of medical doctrine as it was available to the layman. That is changing. There is less awe and greater understanding of the state of medical arts. There is also a growing consciousness that the individual is and should be largely responsible for the state of his or her own health. As many people become aware of the nature of health and its relationship to one's consciousness and lifestyle, and as the choices of types of health care expand and information about them is more available, educated personal choice is becoming more possible. This bodes well for positive societal transformation, as we are beginning to understand physical health, mental health and spiritual health are interrelated.

It is a common understanding, reinforced by the American Medical Association, that we have in the United States the best "state of the art" health care in the world. In the category of biomedicine, or what we think of as conventional medicine, this is most probably the truth. However, health care costs have skyrocketed and fewer and fewer people have access to adequate care. Compared to $4 billion in 1940, by 1992 U.S. health care costs have ballooned to more than $800 billion, and has continued to rise. According to recent statistics, 44 million Americans have no health insurance at all, and another 22 million have inadequate health care coverage. A large proportion of both groups are children.

The growing dependency on high-tech medicine has not only been a factor in rising cost, but in some ways has caused the system to become less responsive to what has been called a health care crisis of chronic disease. Although biomedicine is extremely effective for treating traumatic injuries, and many marvelous technologies have been developed for dealing with various diseases, many patients are discouraged with the growing reliance on the prescription pad and "magic bullet" solutions, in preference to a total holistic (whole body) approach to healing. The medical establishment has also shown an appalling lack of interest in preventive methods as well as in the power of diet to enhance or destroy health.

At the same time, for perhaps the last 40 years, alternative medical therapies have been growing steadily in acceptance and use. Alternative medicine makes use of healing arts from both the Eastern and Western traditions. Most of them are considered holistic, working more naturally within the body's own healing system, and many alternative therapies make use of the mind/body connection. Alternative therapies are less expensive, non-invasive, and usually non-toxic to the system. Some medical systems, such as the Chinese which is alternative to us in the West, are time-honored and have been proven effective in their native cultures. Others have recently been put to systematic scientific testing with results that have had an impact on the practice of our traditional medicine.

In 1992, Congress established the Office of Alternative Medicine (OAM), within the auspices of the National Institute of Health, to facilitate the fair scientific evaluation of alternative therapies that could serve the health and well being of the populace. According to a 1993 article in the *New England Journal of Medicine*, more than 33% of the American people preferred alternative medical treatments over conventional methods, especially for certain conditions, while most Americans used alternative medical therapies in addition to conventional treatments.

There have been several milestones along the path of renewed interest in alternative medicine. The publication of *Anatomy of an Illness* by Norman Cousins in 1979, in which he documented his successful fight against a crippling disease labeled by his doctors as incurable, has had a tremendous impact by bringing alternative therapies to the attention of mainstream Americans. Long time editor of the prestigious *Saturday Review of Literature*, and active in the international arena as president of the World Federalist Association, Cousins was much admired for his intellect and integrity.

Not taking the physician's evaluation of the outcome of his condition as final, Cousins researched the background of his disease and determined the medicine he had been given was counterproductive. He also determined that stress and fatigue were at least partially responsible for the onset of his disease. Cousins luckily found a doctor willing to work with him to mobilize his own body's healing resources. Part of his therapy consisted of mega doses of vitamin C and laughter. With the addition of appropriate medical care, a powerful will and courage, he overcame the disease.

This experience fueled his passion to demonstrate scientifically how the empowerment of the body/mind relationship, working together with traditional medicine, can be a force in overcoming illness. Because of this overriding interest, Cousins left *The Saturday Review* and accepted an appointment to the faculty of the School of Medicine at U.C.L.A. Ten years later Cousins published *Head First: The Biology of Hope*, which describes his quest to document the body/mind relationship through his research and that of his colleagues. His work, as well as that of others, has amply demonstrated that positive attitudes are in fact biochemical realities—that panic, depression, hate, fear, and frustration can have negative effects on human health. At the same time, "hope, faith, love, will-to-live, festivity and playfulness, are powerful biochemical prescriptions."[11] //2

It has long been accepted by the majority of the medical community that heart disease, which results in fatty plaque deposits in the arteries, cannot be physically reversed without surgery, or more recently, in less severe cases, angioplasty. However, in 1988, cardiologist Dean Ornish made known the results of his work with heart disease, setting its treatment on a new, more hopeful path. He demonstrated that the forty patients in his study, through diet and lifestyle changes, had actually been able not only to stop the progress of the disease, but actually to reverse it by shrinking fatty plaque deposits in their arteries. As the patients' arteries began to open, oxygen was again able to reach the heart, and they no longer suffered from chest pain. Instead of surgery, Ornish used therapies that worked with the natural healing power of the body, combining diet and life style changes incorporating such activities as meditation, yoga, exercise and group therapy. Ornish describes his program in a book published in 1990, entitled *Dr. Dean Ornish's Program for*

Reversing Heart Disease.

M3

For the last dozen years, Deepak Chopra has been a leading guru of alternative medicine. Trained in both India and the United States, Dr. Chopra is an endocrinologist and former Chief of Staff of New England Memorial Hospital in Stoneham, Massachusetts.

Moved to investigate further the power of the mind/body relationship that he saw evidenced in his practice, Dr. Chopra returned to his native India to explore Ayurveda, India's ancient healing tradition. The insights he found in Ayurvedic medicine, combined with the best of western medicine, comprise what Dr. Chopra calls a "quantum" method of healing. In his book, *Quantum Healing*, Chopra has brought together the current research of Western medicine, neuroscience and physics with the wisdom of Ayurvedic theory to form a synthesis that enriches our understanding of cause and effect in illness. According to Chopra, "the mind and body are like parallel universes," and "your body is the physical picture, in 3D, of what you are thinking."[112]

Both Chopra and Cousins emphasize the importance of the doctor/patient relationship to the progress of the patient. According to Chopra, numerous studies have shown "that people who trust their doctor and surrender themselves to his care are likelier to recover than those who approach medicine with distrust, fear and antagonism."[113] Also, it has been demonstrated that the doctor's negative evaluation of a patient's condition often works as a self-fulfilling prophecy, while a realistic but hopeful attitude on the part of the physician encourages patients to beat the odds.

Chopra has found, as have Cousins and many others, that the extraordinary ability of the body to heal itself can be facilitated by positive mental attitudes, including a strong will to live, positive emotions, and a lifestyle that modifies stress and encourages relaxation. Chopra feels that "a level of total, deep relaxation is the most important precondition for curing any disorder."[114] Along with conventional medicine when it is needed, he advises therapies, such as meditation, that encourage returning the body back to balance and which facilitate bringing the day-to-day existence to a settled, restful state, thus building a foundation for healing. Chopra calls the living body "the best pharmacy ever devised," which under the proper conditions, and with the proper diet, produces the biochemicals suitable to treat illness in the body. Dr. Bernie Siegel, in *Peace Love and Healing*, agrees and states that "chemicals we produce in our own brains, will become the basis of many therapies of the future."

In *Unconditional Life: Mastering the Forces that Shape Personal Reality*, Dr.Chopra further pursues the thesis that we shape our own reality by the content and force of our consciousness. He recommends the ultimate cure, one which has been a recurring theme throughout these pages: "All of us are radiating our awareness out into the world and bringing its reflection back to us. If your awareness contains violence and dread, you will meet those qualities 'out there.' On the other hand, if your awareness contains unconditional love, the world … will mirror that love. The curative value of this kind of awareness is enormous …."[115]

Dr. Chopra has, for the most part, given up his personal practice in order to write and lecture widely. Dr. Larry Dossey, also an important participant in the transformation to a new philosophy of medicine, calls Dr. Chopra one of the architects of the new medicine in which mind, consciousness, meaning and intelligence play key roles. Dr. Chopra has not discarded the physically-based approach to medicine, but going beyond it, he draws on both modern science and ancient wisdom.

Dr. Bernie S. Siegel is another major figure in the transformation of the healing arts, whose books *Love, Medicine, and Miracles* and *Peace Love and Healing*, have made a major impact on public perception and the professional practice of medicine. He, too, believes that modern medicine, alternative therapies and self-healing are not mutually exclusive, and stresses the relationship between mental and physical health, as well as the potential for the body to cure itself under the right conditions.

Bernie Seigel has come to believe through his experiences as a physician, as well as through the developments of scientific investigation, that there is a healing system that constitutes a sort of superintelligence within us. "Just as that healing system can be set in motion by self-affirming beliefs, self-negating or repressive emotion patterns can do the reverse." Similar to what Chopra calls a restful state conducive to healing, Seigel recommends seeking peace of mind "which will give your healing system a true, 'live' message."[116] Among the many consciousness-altering techniques that are available, he mentions hypnotic suggestion, biofeedback, relaxation training, visualization and yoga, as well as meditation, prayer and music. Beyond the many physiological benefits of meditation, Seigel also emphasizes the spiritual healing that accompanies it.

As did the other great men and women we have quoted in these chapters, Bernie Seigel finds love, love of self and love of others, as well as the realization of our true reality, to be the ultimate answer. "Just as I believe that love and laughter and peace of mind are physiologic, so I also believe that in our earth lives we exist as physical manifestations of the loving, intelligent energy that we call God."[117]

Another physician who has been in the forefront of alternative methods of health and healing is Andrew Weil, M.D. He has caught the public's imagination with his PBS televised lectures on health maintenance, and has written several acclaimed books such as *Health and Healing, Natural Health, Natural Medicine: a Comprehensive Manual for Wellness and Self-care,* and *Spontaneous Healing: How to Discover and Enhance your Body's Natural Ability to Maintain and Heal Itself.* Dr. Weil is eclectic in his approach and recommends a synthesis of conventional and alternative medical treatment.

There are several major fields in alternative medicine and various methods of practice for each. The following will explain the relevance of each, and touch briefly on the more mainstream therapies included in each field of practice.

MIND-BODY INTERVENTION
The Placebo Effect

The interrelationship between the mind and the body has long been intuited, and has even been obvious in some cases to the observing eye. However, new awareness of two types of phenomena has catapulted it to the attention of the medical community: the placebo effect, and the physical and mental changes that occur in cases of multiple personality dramatically and undeniably illustrate the mind/body connection.

The placebo is an inactive substance or preparation given to satisfy the patient's expectations or perceived need for drug therapy, and is also used in controlled studies to determine the efficacy of a medical substance. Norman Cousins and his associates at U.C.L.A. Medical School, interested in showing how the human mind converts ideas and expectations into biochemical realities, explored the phenomena of the placebo. Their studies show dramatic results, and document significant bodily changes as a result of mental processes.[118]

In one study, 411 patients were to receive chemotherapy and were informed to expect hair loss. Thirty percent of the patients were given a placebo instead of chemotherapy, and still experienced hair loss.

Dr. Neil Miller, one of the world's leading experts on behavior medicine, is quoted by Cousins as saying "what is most significant about the placebo response is the proof it offers that thoughts or expectations can be converted into physiological reality."[119] In other words, as Cousins remarks, "belief affects biology."

The interaction of mind/body within the person who

exhibits the multiple personality syndrome is quite startling. For instance, one personality can have diabetes and be insulin deficient while another can immediately shift to a normal blood sugar level. One personality can be allergic to substances that another personality finds harmless. A shift of personality can require the use of heavy glasses, while the other has 20/20 vision.

A new term, and indeed a new field of medicine, called psychoneuroimmunology, is concerned with the complex interactions among the nervous system, the endocrine system and the immune system. The most significant information that has come from this field is the definite knowledge that the immune system is subject to the vagaries of the mind/body connection, as Norman Cousins points out so vividly.

> The immune system can be affected by biochemical changes in the body, by an invasion of microorganisms, by toxicity, by hormonal forces, by emotions, by behavior, by diet, or by a combination of all these factors in varying degrees. The immune system is a mirror to life, responding to its joys and anguish, its exuberance and boredom, its laughter and tears, its excitement and depression, its problems and prospects.[120]

All in all, what we have learned about the mind/body connection could be the most important knowledge we have gleaned in the twentieth century because of its momentous implications. It is certainly one more indication that our consciousness creates our reality.

Meditation

Drs. Deepak Chopra and Bernie Siegel, as well as many others, suggest that meditation is important in the prevention of disease and the maintenance of good health. Various studies have found that regular meditation reduces health care use, increases longevity and quality of life, reduces chronic pain, anxiety, high blood pressure, and lowers blood cholesterol brought on by stress. Deepak Chopra reported that a "1986 Blue Cross-Blue Shield insurance study based on 2000 meditators in Iowa showed that they were much healthier than the American population as a whole in seventeen major areas of serious disease, both mental and physical."[121]

Prayer

Prayer has a mind/body implication both for the person praying and for the prayer recipient. There has been a resurgence of interest in prayer as a healing technique since recent studies have indicated the efficacy of its use. In fact, it has become so mainstream that it has made many local newspapers, as well as the March 1997 cover of *Newsweek* with the article "The Mystery of Prayer." Recently in the *Beacon News* of Aurora, Illinois, a story entitled "Prayer Can Help" reported that Dr. Herbert Benson, Harvard Medical School professor, asserted that prayer can trigger physiologic changes in prayer recipients. The *Newsweek* article cites a longitudinal study being done in the Arthritis Treatment Center in Clearwater, Florida, in which early results show that some individual patients have experienced extraordinary results from prayer. In his recent book *Healing Words*, Dr. Larry Dossey cites the laboratory experiments done by the Spindrift organization in Salem, Oregon that demonstrate that prayer is effective. It is now evident that spirituality and faith have become important aspects of medical practice. In March of 1999, Harvard Medical School joined with The Mind/Body Medical Institute to sponsor a conference entitled "Spirituality and Healing In Medicine."

Yoga

Yoga, meaning union, is an ancient East Indian technique that produces a state of inner harmony and spiritual growth. There are many kinds of yoga but the one usually thought of in the context of alternative healing is hatha yoga, which is a physical discipline consisting of a series of asanas (positions) assumed by the body while concentrating on breathing. The practice of hatha yoga keeps the spine supple and systematically exercises all of the body's muscle groups. This strengthens the organs by increasing respiration and blood flow.

Visualization

Visualization or imagery is a mental process used to encourage changes in attitudes, behavior, and/or physiologic conditions. In some instances, it has been used successfully along with traditional medicine to treat cancer patients.

Biofeedback

Biofeedback uses monitoring instruments to give patients feedback about body processes that can then be used, with practice, to monitor or change or control them. It has been highly successful in the treatment of high blood pressure.

Other mind/body therapies which have been used successfully are psychotherapy, support groups, and laughter and humor. Mind/body therapies are often used along with conventional medical practices to enhance their effectiveness.

ALTERNATIVE SYSTEMS OF MEDICAL PRACTICE

The discussion following will include only those systems for which there is professional practitioner training and standards of practice that are both time tested and can claim scientifically verified outcomes.

Traditional Chinese Medicine

Traditional Chinese medicine is a system comprised of many methods and techniques with a range of application from health promotion to treatment of illness. Whereas the west developed its medical system around the concept of the separation of mind and body, the Eastern approach considers the whole person (mind body and spirit) as well as all of nature to be systemically related. The Chinese practitioner is trained in acupuncture, remedial massage and herbal medicine. The Chinese system also makes use of therapies involving breath, movement and meditation as well as diet to simultaneously treat ailments and maintain health. The prevention of disease and maintenance of good health are the highest goals.

An ancient Chinese practice, acupuncture is applied for anesthesia and to correct an imbalance of life energy (chi) by using tiny needles to direct chi to organs or functions of the body. The acupuncturist does this by selecting points along the body's fourteen meridians that affect the functioning of specific organs, and then using needles to slightly puncture and stimulate bodily tissue at these locations. This procedure does not draw blood nor cause pain. In acupressure, a form of acupuncture, fingers and thumbs rather than needles are used to press chi points on the surface of the body. The World Health Organization recognizes more than forty medical problems, ranging from allergies to arthritis and AIDS, that can be helped by acupuncture treatment.

Herbal prescriptions cover the entire range of of medical ailments and are compounded to have very specific interactions with the body. The pharmacopoeia of Chinese herbalists consists of over 3000 herbs, plus mineral and animal extracts.

Massage as a form of physiotherapy has been taught to Chinese physicians for thousands of years. It is used not only for physical therapy but to treat chronic illness, and in China today every medical student must study massage for two years. The traditional Chinese massage systems, anmo and tuina, employ a complex series of hand movements on specific body parts to produce the desired effects. The

Japanese have adapted the Chinese massage methods into what is now called Shiatsu, which consists of the strong perpendicular application of pressure to the acupuncture points.

Ayurvedic Medicine

The traditional medical practice of India, ayurvedic treats the whole person, not merely the disease, stressing a holistic approach to health. Optimal health is achieved by cultivating mental and physical habits conducive to physical and spiritual well-being, and treatment often includes lifestyle interventions such as hatha yoga, meditation, and natural therapies, especially diet.

Homeopathic Medicine

Practiced worldwide and especially popular in Europe, homeopathy is a system of medicine that treats disease by the administration of minute, extremely diluted, doses of a remedy or substance that would cause the disease in a healthy person. It is based on the law of similars that "like cures like." Homeopathic remedies, made from naturally occurring plant, animal or mineral substances, are recognized and regulated by the Food and Drug Administration and are manufactured under strict guidelines. Homeopathy is used to treat acute and chronic health problems as well as for disease prevention and health promotion. + other

Other alternative systems include anthroposophically extended medicine, naturopathic medicine and environmental medicine. Altogether, these professional health systems provide the thoughtful patient, willing to research his or her illness or disease, the possibility of alternatives to conventional treatment.

MANUAL AND PHYSICAL HEALING METHODS

Touch and manipulation with the hands is an ancient healing practice. Today we are seeing scientific verification of its validity and a broadening of the techniques available for healing the body with physical means. Osteopathy and Chiropractic Medicine have become mainstream. **Osteopathy** requires training identical to that required for an M.D. Traditionally, however, it puts more emphasis on the connection between the structure and function of the body, and therefore practitioners use hands-on procedures more often to identify and relieve illness.

Chiropractic is also concerned with the relationship between structure and function of the human body, especially between the spine and the nervous system, and uses manual techniques in order to restore and preserve health. Many of today's common chiropractic procedures are refinements of methods developed during the past half-century, both in diagnosis and in therapy. Two schools of chiropractic have developed: one that remains with the basic manipulation theory of the past, and one that sees an expanding, more holistic role for the practitioner in the total health of the patient.

Massage Therapy

As previously mentioned, massage therapy consists of manual techniques to manipulate the soft tissues of the body, and is an integral part of Chinese medicine. Although it has also been traditionally used in Western medical practice, as a therapy it fell largely into disuse as modern practice became more influenced by biomedicine and technology. Lately, however, there has been renewed interest from the alternative medical field. Recent studies have shown massage to be very effective in many areas, including relieving stress and depression, fostering relaxation and a generally enhanced state of well being as well as the treatment of back problems. It has also been effective with premature, low birth weight, and cocaine-exposed babies. There are several types of massage available, with varying techniques. **Reflexology** is a foot massage technique that uses "zone therapy" in which specific "zones" on the feet are related to specific organs. As the foot is massaged, pressure is put on these zones which results in the breaking up of tiny crystals which block the energy to the specific organ. Positive results have been reported with reduction of pain, dissolution of kidney stones, recovery from the effects of stroke, sinusitis, sciatica, as well as other disorders.

Rolfing, a deep massage technique developed by Ida Rolf, uses deep manipulation of the connective tissue (fascia) to restore the body's natural alignment, which may have become rigid through injury, emotional trauma and inefficient movement habits.

There are several body techniques that seek to correct postural and functional disorders caused by stresses and strains of the body due to consistent physical habits of movement, poor posture, and emotional tensions. The **Feldenkrais** method uses two therapies. "Awareness through movement" is a verbally-directed method of gentle exploratory movement sequences organized around a specific function, such as reaching or bending, with the intention of increasing awareness of multiple possibilities of action. "Functional integration" involves the use of words and gentle, noninvasive touch to guide an individual student to an awareness of existing and alternative movement patterns. The **Alexander** technique is a system of body dynamics that includes movements that improve balance, posture, and coordination and relieve pain. **Trager psychophysical integration** seeks to ease movement, loosen joints, and release chronic patterns of tension by means of light, rhythmic rocking and shaking movements.

HERBAL MEDICINES

Literally all cultures world-wide have traditions in herbal medicine. According to the World Health Organization, 80% of the world population currently use herbal medicine for at least some part of their health care. It is estimated that over

30% of our modern drugs are of herbal origin. In the United States, many people who have become leery of the overprescribed, expensive pharmaceutical drugs are turning to herbal medicine as being both less expensive and less toxic. With renewed interest, more information about the most efficacious use of herbs is available. In l981 the U.S.D.A., in conjunction with the National Cancer Institute, concluded a 75 year study of plants with possible anticancer properties. The final work included a list of 365 folk medicinal species and identifies more than 1,000 pharmacologically active phytochemicals, potentially beneficial to humanity. A pressing world-wide concern, however, is the loss of plant species being destroyed at alarming rates. Although in 2001 the statistics are not in, it has been predicted that in the United States an estimated 10% of all species of flowering plants would be extinct by the year 2000. Every day during the devastation of the rain forests abundant species are being destroyed.

DIET AND NUTRITION

Diet and nutrition are at last receiving the attention they deserve as a means of maintaining good health, and in the prevention and treatment of chronic disease. As more and more studies have documented the relationship between diet, health and the development of certain diseases, the medical establishment is slowly catching up with what has been long obvious to many in the alternative movement. There is no longer any doubt that the "privileged" diet of the technologicaly developed societies, characterized by an excess of foods rich in animal fat, partially hydrogenated vegetable oils, and refined carbohydrates, but lacking in fresh fruits and vegetables and whole grains, is causing adverse health effects. Study after study, as well as comparisons of cultures, indicate that meat and dairy products can be dangerous to our health.

During World War I, when Denmark was cut off from

imports, the nation's grain was fed to the people, not the livestock. At the end of the war, startling results showed that during the year when food restrictions were most severe and the people were eating a diet of grains, the overall mortality rate fell by 34% from the preceding 18 years. Several studies have found strong correlations between heavy meat-eating cultures and short life expectancy, with the reverse for vegetarian cultures. Many experts are now suggesting that the diet most recommended to avoid heart disease and cancer is one of fresh vegetables, fruit, legumes and whole grains, with perhaps a small amount of fish (although it is so hard to find fish uncontaminated with toxins that pregnant women are now instructed to avoid fish completely).

More than ever, such a diet is in accord with the law of the universe "as above so below"; what is good for one part of God's creation is good for all. U.S. agribusiness has devised ways of raising livestock that squeezes every dollar from the sale of their flesh, while the suffering these animals undergo has become so extreme it is almost unbelievable.* As John Robbins states in *Diet for a New America*, "… the very eating habits that can do so much to give you strength and health are exactly the same ones that can significantly reduce the needless suffering in the world, and do so much to preserve our ecosystem."[122]

Not only people suffer the effects of agribusiness. Pigs are crammed for a lifetime into cages in which they can hardly move, forced against their natures to stand in their own waste until it is disposed of. And what happens to the waste that in the past, when hogs were raised outside, fertilized the soil? According to an article in a Sierra Club publication, "Iowa, Minnesota, Missouri and North Carolina are trying now to clean up more than 42 million gallons of hog waste spills from mega farms. The total number of spills … is catastrophic. In addition, they are trying to deal with the random dumping of dead animals." In order to keep the animals alive under deplorable conditions, they are continually plied with antibiotics and other drugs. They still lose some.

We are also feeling the results of this practice, as strains of bacteria develop that are resistant to drugs fed to livestock. As a result, diseases that used to be treatable in humans with antibiotics are becoming more dangerous. Add the pesticides that go into livestock feed and the hormones into their bodies, and the meat rendered is increasingly unhealthy.** The U. S. National Academy of Sciences estimates that one million cases of cancer over the next decade will result from pesticide poisoning in food, and there is alarming evidence that the hormone supplements given to animals are causing our children to develop sexually at a premature age.

Another change taking place in the health field is in the attitudes about the appropriateness of supplemental vitamins and minerals. Although some physicians still claim that you don't need vitamin supplements, their number decreases year by year. Until recently, most medical doctors had little or no training in nutrition. According to a report made to the National Institute of Health, there is a growing body of data to support the claims by many health professionals that the RDAs recommended for a health-preserving diet are not adequate and supplements may be necessary. There is also increasing evidence that the therapeutic use of high doses of vitamins can be effective in treating some chronic diseases. Supplements of vitamins and minerals as well as alternative diets are more often being recommended for their healing value and as a preventive measure.

Diet holds the most promise of all as we turn to new ways to enhance our health and prevent disease. Dr. Gio B. Gori, the Deputy Director of the National Cancer Institute's Division of Cancer Cause and Prevention made the following testimony to a Senate committee: "Nutritional science is coming of age ... No other field of research seems to hold better promise for the prevention and control of cancer and other illnesses, and for securing and maintaining human health."

Although the above discussion does not include all the alternatives available to either replace or supplement traditional medicine, it does give an idea of the new and encouraging directions in which health care is moving. Our enhanced understanding of the mind/body connection gives us what Norman Cousins calls a "biology of hope." Indeed, Deepak Chopra suggests that "insofar as it can change your participation in disease, every system [of medical therapy] is capable of working." That participation now includes a choice of a number of alternative and/or supplements to traditional medicine. The new focus on holistic medicine encourages the traditional practitioner to employ therapies out of his domain to augment his own treatment, and also the alternative practitioner to call upon traditional medical science and technology when needed. In his book *The Other Medicines*, Richard Grossman urges a "stronger, deeper, and more sustained consideration of the possibility of complementarity" between health care practices.[123] That is beginning to happen now.

After years of controversy, insurance companies and HMO's are showing interest in alternative therapies due to the financial incentives. To explore the possibility of saving a great deal of money, Mutual of Omaha did a study in which they allowed several hundred subscribers to participate in a program developed by Dr. Dean Ornish to show that a lifestyle-based regimen could not only prevent heart disease but reverse it. Mutual of Omaha has now arranged a program for their participants that can eventually save up to $20 for each insurance dollar they spend with Ornish. Other companies are following suit. Sharp Health Plan, an HMO in California, offers subscribers an eight-session wellness course designed by Dr. Deepak Chopra. American Western Life has launched a program called a Prevention Plus and Wellness Plan. The trend is widening.

It is possible that with the reduction of health care costs resulting from lifestyle changes, including healthful diet and exercise, and use of less expensive alternative therapies when appropriate, enough resources would be freed to enable us to have excellent health care for all our children, prenatal care for all expectant mothers, and state of the art medical treatment and technology available for those who need it.

*For a detailed account of these practices, see *Diet for a New America*, by John Robbins.

**For a detailed account of the environmental effects of intensive farming of hogs and cattle, see *Diet for a New America* by John Robbins.

CHAPTER EIGHT

THE CHANGING FACE
OF ECONOMICS

> We are living through one of the most fundamental shifts in history—a change in the actual belief structure of Western society. No economic, political, or military power can compare with the power of a change of mind. By deliberately changing their images of reality, people are changing the world.
>
> *Willis Harman*, Global Mind Change

Adam Smith, who published *The Wealth of Nations* in 1776, is the acknowledged father of modern economics. His main premise, that individuals acting in their own self-interest would promote the common good, instituted a confusion of means and ends that continues to distort what has come to be called "economic good." Smith, greatly influenced by the then new mechanistic theories of science, based his ideas about the "free market" and "division of labor" on Newtonian theory.

The Newtonian view of the universe was one of isolated, separate atoms whose actions, guided by deterministic forces, could be studied and predicted in a fixed and law-abiding, and we now know, fictional universe. Danah Zohar, in *The*

Quantum Society, writes that the political and economic thinkers of Smith's time "compared these colliding atoms and their interacting forces to the behavior and interactions of individuals in society as they confront each other in the pursuit of their self interest."[124] Darwin's theory of the survival of the fittest gave further impetus to the belief in deterministic forces.

The 19th century Utilitarian Movement, whose main proponents were Jeremy Bentham, John Stuart Mill, and Herbert Spencer, promoted a compatible idea to Adam Smith's theory that pleasure is the basic motivating force of humanity and empiricism should be the source of all knowledge. Although admittedly the main concern of Utilitarianism was to foster a "good" society that would maximize pleasure and minimize pain for the greatest number, their psychology, based on evolution theory and Newtonian mechanics, was fundamentally flawed.

The dominance of the Newtonian reductionist scientific materialism, in operation for more than a century, has had profound consequences throughout society. When there is a dominant view of the nature of reality, that view tends to permeate every aspect of our lives, our belief systems and our institutions. The view of scientific materialism melded with masculine values to take science in mixed directions, producing amazing breakthroughs, and technological development not necessarily grounded in humane values.

The reductionist mind-set of the Newtonian scientific paradigm has also had a significant impact on the theory and practice of economics. In her book *Paradigms in Progress*, economist Hazel Henderson describes some of the effects of the misguided use of the reductionist philosophy in both science and economics. "Today, the powerful and often unintended, consequences of this narrow view of reality [reductionism] are unavoidable: polluted skies, toxic dumps, oil spills, advancing deserts, shrinking forests, broken families and communities, and millions of neglected children, 40,000 of whom die every day from starvation, millions of others malnourished or roaming the streets of cities, homeless and abandoned."[125] Add to that list acid rain, depletion of our soils, global warming, the insidious and ubiquitous chemical toxins that have invaded every aspect of our lives, threatening our very survival as a species, and they all add up to what Willis Harmon, late Director of the Institute of Noetic Sciences, calls the "macroproblem" which faces not only each country but the global community.

The main problem with the prevailing economic paradigm is that it deals with goods and services in accordance with their market value and not in accordance with what they are. Market value is often influenced by marketing and advertising practices designed to play upon human ignorance and vulnerability rather than to educate for real needs. Traditional economic theory does not suggest that the costs of producing and marketing a product should take account of "free goods" such as air, water, soil and the whole framework of living nature. At the same time, the tools of economic judgment, the GNP (Gross National Product) and the GDP (Gross Domestic Product), count all that is spent on final goods and services currently produced, no matter for what purpose, as growth in the economy, and therefore deemed good. No difference is made between consumption of oranges or money spent to clean up an oil spill or a river filled with toxic waste.

The biggest sin in the traditional economist's opinion is to do something "uneconomic." The late E. F. Schumacher, an economist himself and author of *Small is Beautiful*, regrets that within the discipline, even though you might "call a thing immoral or ugly, soul-destroying or a degradation of man, a peril to the peace of the world or the well-being of future generations, as long as you have not shown it to be 'uneconomic' you have not really questioned its right to exist, grow and prosper."[126] Tom Chappell, a modern day businessman who wrote *The Soul of a Business: Managing for*

Profit and the Common Good, agrees that the traditional attitude of business is that "profit is King ...."

"Traditionally in the business world," Chappell writes, "'the right move' is weighted only according to how profitable it is. If using cheaper material increases profit, if polluting the air and rivers increases profits, then so be it."[127]

Schumacher points out that the modern industrial system, a product of scientific technology and economic theory, "consumes the very basis on which it has been erected ... It lives on irreplaceable capital which it cheerfully treats as income."[128] It voraciously consumes fossil fuels, the natural environment and the human substance. The more successful the industrial society becomes in promoting production and consumption, the shorter its life span will be. Richard Barrett of the World Bank states very forcefully in an article entitled "Reformulating Values in an Interdependent World," "The economy is a wholly owned subsidiary of the environment. When the environment is finally forced to file for bankruptcy because its resource base has been polluted, degraded, and irretrievably compromised, then the economy will go bankrupt with it."[*]

As the economic theory and the practices of many businesses and industrialists are being called to account, a new realization is beginning to dawn, even in some conservative circles. A 1989 survey of the environment, "Costing the Earth," published by the prestigious journal, *The Economist,* draws the following conclusions:

> At present, most economic activity takes little account of the costs it imposes on its surroundings. Factories pollute rivers as if the rinsing water flowed past them for free, power stations burn coal without charging customers for the effects of carbon dioxide belched into the atmosphere, loggers destroy forests without a care for the impact on wildlife or climate. These bills are left for others to pick up—neighbors,

citizens of other countries and future generations …. Conventional statistics of economic growth are … particularly blind to the environment. National income accounts take no notice of the value of natural resources: a country that cut down all its trees, sold them as wood chips and gambled away the money … would appear from its national accounts to have got richer in term of GNP per person. *citation source*

Such values are seldom consciously espoused by most people, yet they have been tacitly accepted as guiding principles in our institutions and often in our private behavior, molded psychologically by the prevailing worldview. As people recognize the disconnection between the prevailing economic paradigm that, among other things, promotes the "consumer society" and identifies human beings as consumers, that encourages materialism with its vacuous rewards, and engenders the destruction of the natural world as it falls victim to the "production" of more things, as they see the disconnection of these values from the deepest desires of their hearts, they will disconnect from the economic paradigm that fosters them. It is already happening.

There is a current movement to change our way of measuring the economy to an indices of GPI, Genuine Progress Indicator, which would use multiple indices to get a more honest view of the health of our national economy. Also, there has been an enormous interest in a PBS documentary, later to come out in book form, entitled *Affluenza*—the term for a "painful, contagious, socially transmitted condition of overload, debt, anxiety and waste resulting from the dogged pursuit of more."[129] In our nation, there is the beginning of the awareness of the prevalence of this "social disease" and a slow turning to a movement of voluntary simplicity.

Although the majority of economists and business people are still operating within the above described economic paradigm, there is a growing number of economists, as well as business and industrial leaders, putting it aside and beginning to develop the theory and practice of a new way of doing business—a way that will bring profit not only to the business, but to the community at large. There is a new theme slowly developing in the business world, "doing well by doing good."

A 1996 Management Development Conference, put together by The Conference Board, a renowned business membership organization, offered sessions that speak to the change beginning to occur in the business world: "Social Responsibility: Transforming the World We Live in," and "Liberating the Corporate Soul: Leadership and Spirituality in the 21st century." In these sessions, such concepts as enlightened leadership, value-centered leadership and the role of spirituality in leadership and organizational life were explored. (Source)

Psychologist Abraham Maslow was among the first to introduce value-centered concepts of management which, thirty years later, are beginning to be taken seriously. On sabbatical from Brandeis University, Maslow studied the work being done in a company called Non-Linear Systems which produced voltmeters in a converted blimp hanger in Del Mar, California. He described the spirit and productivity of the plant in his journal later published as the book *Eupsychian Management*. Maslow was setting a new trend when used the terms "enlightened management"—management that provides conditions and leadership to promote self-actualization and the achievement of potential in the workplace, and "synergy," the extra energy and productivity that comes from cooperation, teamwork and trust.

There are many books now available about concepts of enlightened business and management that work to bring success to the business and dignity to the workers, while not despoiling the environment or using excessive resources. One such book, *The Soul of a Business* by Tom Chappell, President of Tom's of Maine, takes the reader step by step through the difficulties and joys of creating such a profitable business.

Chappell was concerned with showing how mind and spirit can work together to compete for profit and market share. He wanted to demonstrate that besides making money, which he felt was important, a business could also be accountable to the beliefs and values of its owners and employees. The following commitment is central to the company's mission statement: "To be a profitable and successful company, while acting in a socially and environmentally responsible manner."

In his relationships with employees and customers, Chappell patterned his policies after the "I/Thou" philosophy of Martin Buber. Chappell wrote that "thinking of a company as simply a collection of jobs being done so that profits can go to the bank turns the company into another version of Buber's "I/It" relationship. It dehumanizes employees, treats them as things, as mere job categories."[130] In this respect, he was also influenced by the teachings of Jonathan Edwards, a preacher in the early American colonies, who believed that we define ourselves by our relationships.

Although often confronted with choices difficult in the face of traditional economic "wisdom," Chappell and his board of directors always made the choice for values, and succeeded beyond their expectations in building a successful business. "Implicit in our faith," wrote Chappell, "is that goodness is flowing all around us, and we're looking for ways to connect to its energy."[131] Every decision made by Tom's of Maine for the "right" rather than the expedient reason paid off bountifully in business growth and profits. The increased profits have allowed the company to be able to reach out more and more to their immediate community as well as the national community in service projects and contributions.

Another publication that has greatly influenced the behavior not only of business people but of the public at large is the celebrated book 7 *Habits of Highly Effective People*, by Stephen R. Covey. The philosophy espoused by Covey, based on time-honored principles, is profoundly moral and spiritual. Covey writes about the significance of an internal paradigm shift when we begin to see the world more clearly than our previous limited "worldview" had allowed. A consciousness shift of this kind, he suggests, brings about a change in behavior.

The principle that Covey includes as Habit 4, "The Principle of Interpersonal Leadership; Think Win/Win," ought to have the deepest implications for our future as it is put into use by more and more people. "Win/Win is a frame of mind and heart that constantly seeks mutual benefit in all human interaction. Win/Win means that agreements or solutions are mutually beneficial, mutually satisfying ... Win/Win is the belief in the Third Alternative. It's not your way or my way; but a better way, a higher way."[132]

Business Consultant Margaret Wheatley is one of the first to write explicitly about the effect on business of the change in worldview brought about by the revelations of quantum physics. She explains in *Leadership and the New Science* how traditional business practices reflect the Newtonian scientific paradigm: "It is interesting to note just how Newtonian most organizations are. The machine imagery of the spheres was captured by organizations in an emphasis on structure and parts. Responsibilities have been organized into functions. People have been organized into roles." She goes on to say, "This reduction into parts and the proliferation of separations has characterized not just organizations, but everything in the world during the past three hundred years."[133] The prime focus of her book is to show how the new science can change the ways we understand, design, lead and manage organizations.

Wheatley has revamped her priorities and skills as a management consultant to many and varied organizations. Now, instead of analyzing parts, she focuses on the whole, on patterns of movement in the organization over time and "qualities like rhythm, flow, direction and shape." She no longer looks for one-to-one cause and effect relationships when analyzing business problems, but toward more dynamic patterns of interrelationships within the whole. According to Wheatley, "The era of the rugged individual has been replaced by the era of the team players. The quantum world has demolished the concept of the unconnected individual … What gives positive power to the organization is the quality of relationships … Love in organizations, then, is the most potent source of power we have available."[134] Love, the most potent force in the universe! How exciting to find it now included in the tenets of good business practice.

There have been many examples in recent years of organizations which have profited from "doing the right thing" socially and/or environmentally. Sometimes the changes in policy have been made through personal choice, and some changes have been forced by circumstances. Often, however, no matter the reason, the results have been surprisingly beneficial to all concerned. What seemed to be untenable to good "economic" practice, turned out to be more profitable in the long run. The following are a few such cases.

One architect with vision and a deep concern about the impending exhaustion of fossil fuels with all its implications has given the world a concrete example of his belief—that business can only profit through conservation. Randolph Croxton, founder and director of Croxton Collaborations, made headlines when he creatively "reused" an 1891 department store building in Manhattan for the "new" National Audubon Society Headquarters. Croxton believes "we have been living by the idea that cheapest is best … Now the bills are coming in for the cleanup, for getting past hydrocarbons, for all the fallout from pollution. We're having to ask, 'What are the economic consequences for what we are doing.'"[135] Croxton's design for the Audubon building made use of available technologies in wall insulation, high efficiency gas-fired heating and air-conditioning systems, windows and skylights, lighting systems, wall and furniture colors, recycled building materials, and other items to create a building that for every dollar spent will save $5.00 in efficiency. Although some initial outlays were more costly than standard building practices would require, according to Croxton, they will pay for themselves in three to five years. The heating and air-conditioning system alone is expected to save $36,000 a year, and the electricity bills should be 80% less than normal. Croxton has demonstrated with the efficient and attractive Audubon building that revamping older buildings is not necessarily less efficient than building new ones.

Dee Hock, one of the preeminent entrepreneurs of the 20th century, founded Visa International in 1970, a non-stock, for-profit corporation cooperatively owned by more than twenty thousand financial institutions worldwide. Now valued at 300 billion dollars, Visa International is so structured that the power resides with the 20,000 institutions; the management has no equity and cannot demand exorbitant compensation. "In Visa," Hock states, "the power resides in the periphery, in the most local part, not in the core."

In 1984, Hock began a self-imposed nine year sabbatical from the business world to think and write about the problems he had encountered in the world, especially as related to institutions. Hock returned to the public arena in 1995 only, he said, for the sake of his grandchildren, with ideas he feels could help to bring about positive institutional change in America. He believes that we are headed for massive institutional failure, largely due to the practices of "Newtonian control and immense centralization of power" in institutions both public and private. The corporation as an institution, Hock says, has changed dramatically from its original purpose, to "achieve a social good beyond the limits of the individual."

> They have gradually freed themselves of all restraint ... For example, all gain increasingly goes to shareholders, ... and not to the community or em-

ployees or customers. At the same time the corporation demands the right to exploit irreplaceable natural resources with minimal payment and to use the biosphere as a free sink for product waste. If a corporation fails, cuts twenty thousand jobs, or moves a plant overseas, the people and communities that supported them don't disappear, they become a social cost ... and have become mechanisms for the capitalization of gain, and the socialization of loss.

He also cites as a major problem the "fact that our wealth and power continues to be concentrated in few and fewer hands."[136]

A devotee of chaos theory as applied to institutions, Hock created The Chaordic Alliance, "a global institution to develop and implement new, more effective, and equitable concepts of commercial, political and social organizations." Hock has outlined the process for creating a chaordic organization, which exists in the "narrow phase between 'chaos' and 'order.'" First, an organization or institution should define its purpose with absolute clarity; then its principles, or fundamental beliefs by which it intends to be guided. After these have been decided, structure follows then people, and then practice.

In 1996, Aaron Feuerstein, a mill owner, made news due to his unusual and seemingly "uneconomic" decisions. The sub-heading in a *Fortune* magazine story ran: "Malden Mills owner Aaron Feuerstein was both ridiculed and canonized when he kept his 1,000 employees on the payroll after a fire burned down his factory last Christmas. But now he's proving that treating workers well is just plain good business." The economic "wisdom" after the fire was that Feuerstein should take the insurance money, close the business and walk away, or else use the insurance money to move the company to a state or country with lower labor costs. However, according to a report by Steve Wulf in *Time* magazine, "Feuerstein, who reads from both his beloved Shakespeare and the Talmud almost every night, has never been one to run away."[137] Instead he chose to think creatively.

On December 14, three days after the fire, he called his employees together and made the pledge: "For the next 30 days, and it may be more—all our employees will be paid their full salaries ... By January 2, we will restart operations, and within 90 days we will be fully operational." Malden Mills has made a profitable comeback due to worker loyalty and a quality product—Polartec, a warm but lightweight fabric, made from recycled plastic bottles. In fact, several customers, such as L. L. Bean, made sizeable contributions to the rebuilding of the plant.

Feuerstein is not against downsizing when it is the legitimate answer to advanced technology. He is against all practices used for short term gains at the cost of human suffering and long term production. Worker loyalty has paid off for Feuerstein; productivity revenues in constant dollars more than tripled from 1982 to 1995, while the work force barely doubled. Thomas Teal, author of the *Fortune* article, writes, "This isn't the work of a saint or a fool, it's the considered and historically successful policy of a genial manufacturing genius who might serve as a model for every man and woman in business."[138]

Another example of a businessman who valued his employees was reported in the August 1, 1999 edition of *The Washington Post*. When Bob Thompson sold his Michigan-based asphalt and paving business for $422 million, he made sure that none of his employees would be laid off because of the sale. Then he informed his 550 employees that he would be sharing $128 million with them. Some became instant millionaires. Thompson remarked that his employees were dedicated workers even under difficult conditions, and he couldn't have been successful without them.

Some businesses and industries become believers only after discovering that they "do well by doing good." The chemical industry accounts for nearly half of the toxic pollution produced in the Unites States, and has, for the most part, been quite unwilling to clean up after itself, claiming "uneconomic" costs. As it turns out, that is not true. Another headline appeared in *The Wall Street Journal* several years ago which stated "Chemical Firms Find That It Pays to Reduce Pollution at Source: By Altering Processes to Yield Less Waste, They Make Production More Efficient."[139]

Although for years Du Pont has been spewing out 110 million pounds of waste annually, they have recently discovered that by adjusting the manufacturing process, they are able to cut down a plant's waste by two-thirds and save one million dollars a year. According to the same article in *The Wall Street Journal*, Dow Chemical has found that by recycling a toxic solvent used to make its Verdict herbicide, they are able to save about three million dollars a year while reducing the waste by half.

There are many other examples of chemical companies finding it profitable to "do the right thing" environmentally. The former Environmental Protection Agency administrator, William Reilly, observed that the entire chemical industry is "getting religion" about the benefits of cutting wastes. Some benefits are coming from increasing production efficiency, others from increased use of by-products. In fact, says Scott McMurray, author of the same *Wall Street Journal* article, chemical companies are beginning to "conclude that pollution was a sign of a bad manufacturing system."

Many utility companies are also finding that it is profitable to go "green." Hazel Henderson writes in *Paradigms in Progress*, "Conservation is at last recognized as seven times more cost-effective than adding new supply." Utility companies, Henderson claims, are finding that "it is cheaper for them to even give their customers efficient light bulbs and shower heads and give them low-interest loans to install good windows and other insulation, than it is to build new power plants."[140] Two of the biggest utility companies, Pacific Gas and Electric of California and New York's Con Edison, have implemented conservation practices. As a test case, Iowa Public Service Co. has decided to equip the homes of a town of 2700 people with the very latest in electricity-saving devices. Minnesota Mining and Manufacturing has made adjustments by changing their production processes through their program "Pollution Prevention Pays."

An important book that documents that business people and businesses can "do well by doing good" has recently been published. *Aiming Higher: 25 Stories of How Companies Prosper by Combining Sound Management And Social Vision* is a study of how the philosophy of business is beginning to change. Movie producer and founder of The Business Enterprise Trust, Norman Lear, remarks in the foreword, "The evidence seems clear that those businesses which actively serve their many constituencies in creative, morally thoughtful ways, also, over the long run, serve their shareholders best. Companies do, in fact, do well by doing good. These are stories," says Lear, "of resourceful men and women who are tackling serious social challenges through their businesses—while helping them thrive."[141]

Not only are businesses and corporations beginning to show signs of positive change, but individuals are beginning to consider the power they have to encourage that change through their investments. According to Hazel Henderson, "One of the best indicators that companies are responding to environmental imperatives with greener products and more socially responsible ways of doing business is the overall growth of the socially-responsible investment movement, up from 40 billion of assets in 1982 to 650 billion in 1991."[142] This type of "clean and green" investing has grown faster than any other market segment. In fact, almost $1.00 out of every $10.00 under financial management today is involved in social investing. Smith Barney makes the following statement in one of its advertisements: "SOCIALLY RESPONSIBLE INVESTING: WE BELIEVE YOU DON'T HAVE TO

SACRIFICE PROFITS FOR PRINCIPLES."

An organization called Co-Op America publishes a journal called *Co-Op America Quarterly* which informs readers about socially responsible investing. They feel it is important "that citizens be empowered with the tools and information that they need to vote with their dollars." The journal calls attention to the particular focus of various mutual funds. For instance, Pax World Fund does not invest in weapons production, nuclear power, or the tobacco or gambling industries, and its ten year growth figures are impressive. According to the article "Can You Really Do Well by Doing Good?," the evidence shows that "over the long term, responsible investors can be expected to do as well or even better than investors who don't consider their values." The above article also quotes a study done by the Investor Responsibility Research Center and Vanderbilt University which affirms the profitability of responsible investing. "The data suggest that firms complying with environmental laws and firms that have relatively cleaner processes than their competitors do well in the stock market ... and 'low pollution' portfolios performed better than the 'high pollution' portfolios."[143] *Co-op Quarterly*

Consumers are also realizing that they can contribute to responsible economic growth through their purchasing power. In former years, we have witnessed successful consumer boycotts of such products as lettuce and grapes in the food industry. More and more people are refusing to participate in the excessively cruel and unhealthy practices of the meat and poultry industries, as reflected in the growth of profits of those using humane methods of production for chickens, beef and hogs. Also, coffee products are now on the market which are not grown on cleared or otherwise sterile slopes.

Consumers are given even more opportunities with socially responsible credit cards, such as Working Assets Visa, which makes sizable contributions to "green" and humane causes. Working Assets also has a telephone company that not only contributes a percentage of profits to causes, but allows the consumers free phone calls to the President and legislators in Washington, D.C. There are now credit cards that support individual organizations from The Sierra Club, American Association of University Women, The United Nations Association, and many others.

It is often pointed out that business is the heartbeat of a society. We might say that when business gets a heart, society might truly flourish. That may not be so far away. Michael Ray, a Stanford University professor of Personal Creativity in Business and a proponent of consciousness in commerce, says that "business is the leading institution in society—the cause of many of the world's problems but also its best source for solutions." He calls for a new model of business whose goal is the enlightenment of everyone within the organization—work that is personally fulfilling as well as socially responsible.[144]

Everywhere, we are finding more evidence of the truth of the metaphysical law that what is good for one is good for all, or what is good for a business, or an institution, is good for the people and the planet. Although sometimes the perils that beset our world seem beyond our power to change, the truth is that we do have many choices to make an important difference.

*On a very hopeful note, Richard Barrett was asked by his colleagues in The World Bank to set up a spiritual study group which turned out to be the start of the Spiritual Unfoldment Society for the World Bank.

**Some have thought the world "gross" in GNP and GDP should be used in its most egregious meaning.

CHAPTER NINE

THE "MACROPROBLEM" AND
THE NEW GROUP OF WORLD SERVERS

"Salvation is a collaborative venture."
The Course in Miracles

There are those who believe that our world's problems have grown to such a magnitude as to be insurmountable and that civilization as we know it is doomed. This belief constitutes a self-fulfilling prophecy, for where there is no hope, there is no action. Others, while not dismissing the dimensions of what Willis Harman calls the "Macroproblem" facing the world, believe that there is always hope where there is will, understanding, and dedication.

Many people believe that civilization as we know it will have to end. It will have to become better, to transcend narrow belief systems and narrow interests, find ways to transform conflict into cooperation, and rise to a higher mental and spiritual plane of human conduct. They believe through a shift in consciousness and thus a shift in direction, we can bring into being a new Age of Spiritual Enlightenment. The science that we have looked at suggests that this transformation is possible, even probable, when a critical mass of human energy is directed to the positive solution of our problems.

Those in the forefront of the movement toward transformation are termed by Alice Bailey, founder of a spiritual education society named Lucis Trust, as "the new group of world servers." She describes them as, "Every man and woman in every country in both hemispheres who is working to heal the breaches between people, to evoke the sense of brotherhood, to foster the sense of mutual interrelation, and who sees no racial, national or religious barriers, ..." These "believers" have already swung into action, and the group is growing day by day. There is certainly no formal association; each person is called individually to serve the common cause in ways that are most appropriate for him or her. They very much resemble Maslow's profile for his "peakers"; those in the process of self-actualization, who are characterized by an ability to love and care from an ego-transcending perspective and are committed to some cause or work outside of themselves. They have been anticipated by the Dalai Lama who said, "It seems like the fate of our civilization will depend upon grass-roots action by partnership-minded groups that are presently in existence, or that will be formed within this decade."

I. THE POVERTY OF RICHES: THE UNITED STATES

The citizens of the United States have long considered their society the most democratic and egalitarian in existence. Americans believe they have a strong and prosperous middle class and an ongoing dedication to reduce, if not eliminate, poverty. For many years, this was perhaps more true than false. However, in recent years there has been an alarming change. A headline in my local Aurora, Illinois paper, *The Beacon News*, read: "Gap between rich and poor widest in U.S., studies indicate." The article went on to document the statement that since the 1970s when economic inequalities began to widen, "the United States has become the most economically stratified of the industrial nations."

Researchers at the Federal Reserve and Internal Revenue

Service reported that in 1976 the richest 1 percent of our population held about 20 percent of the nation's household wealth. By 2000, the richest 1 percent held 40 percent. The top fifth of our population gets nearly half of the wealth—49 percent, while the poorest fifth gets less than 4 percent. These figures show the most uneven distribution of wealth among all industrial nations. *Source*

The increase of poverty in the United States has its deepest effects on children. It is, of course, a cliche to say that our future depends on our children, but most cliches are true. Luckily, our children have a mighty force working in their favor in the person of Marian Wright Edelman. Raised in a close-knit community in Bennettsville, South Carolina, her life of service began early when she and her siblings tended to the residents of a nursing home for African Americans started by her father, a Baptist minister. She remembers a close, supportive community of adults which served as buffer against the harsh realities of poverty and segregation. Her parents, teachers and church leaders taught her never to give up in the face of adversity. And she doesn't.

Edelman was the first black woman to be admitted to the Mississippi state bar. After marrying Peter Edelman in 1973, they moved to Washington D.C., where she founded the Children's Defense Fund. By keeping the facts about the state of America's children before the face of the administration and Congress as well as the general public, she has become the most powerful advocate for children in America. According to Edelman, in her article "Children Under Siege," "the state of American children is in crisis. With fifteen million children living in poverty, ten million with no health insurance, they are also the victims of violence, shattered homes, poor nutrition and inadequate education." Edelman makes a strong point when she says, "Surely the world's mightiest military power can keep its children safe. Surely the world's richest nation can keep its children from being poor citizens." *source*

Another advocate for children is former First Lady, Hillary Rodham Clinton. She has provided valuable information about the state of our children and the prospects for their well being in her book *It Takes A Village*. To explain this concept, Mrs. Clinton writes, "The children are cradled in the family, which is primarily responsible for their passage from infancy to adulthood. But around the family are the larger settings of neighborhood, school, church, workplace, community, culture, economy, society, nation and world, which affect children directly or through the well-being of their families."[145] Her words are underscored in a pastoral letter by the United States Catholic Conference entitled "Putting Children and Families first." "The undeniable fact is that our children's future is shaped both by the values of their parents and the policies of our nations." *Source*

There is a bright side to our national picture. Many remarkable people are working within their local communities and throughout the nation to make their "village" a better, safer, more compassionate, nurturing place. They are working to alleviate poverty and hunger, to house the homeless, to ensure a non-toxic, more benign environment, to reduce violence and abuse, to foster education and psychological well-being. They are working as political and social advocates, as well as in the trenches of personal service. They are called from many walks of life, from the affluent to the destitute, from religious and lay perspectives. They are marked by the sense of joy they receive from their work and the inner peace that comes from the confidence that they are doing the work their souls require.

One such person is Mother Waddles of Detroit, Michigan, who has been called a "one woman war on poverty." Charleszetta Waddles established The Perpetual Mission for Saving Souls of All Nations, which, during its 30 years of existence, has become an important part of the Detroit social welfare system. An ordained minister, Mother Waddles tells her congregation that her mission is "to the young, old, black, white, rich, poor, drunk and sober" and to "love the hell out of them."[146] The Mission provides food, clothing, furniture, emergency assistance, housing referrals, tutoring, legal services and vocational education classes. Besides this, Mother Waddles provides information about community services to those in need through a radio program called "Radio Help." She also administers a prison and jail ministry.

Through a series of difficulties, Charleszetta was left the sole support of her family when she was twelve. Then after several failed marriages, she had to draw on all of the resourcefulness at her command to create a decent life for her children and herself. She worked two or three jobs at a time, kept house, and tried to be creative in feeding her children inexpensive yet appetizing food.

At the age of 42, still living in poverty, Charleszetta began her mission which grew out of a women's Bible study group. Their goal was to provide those things most needed in the community, following Christ's exhortation to feed the hungry and clothe the naked. Charleszetta felt that a person was never too poor to help someone else.

For her work, Mother Waddles has received many awards, including the Distinguished Citizen Award from Michigan State and Wayne State University, special tributes by the state of Michigan, the Community Service Award from the Ford Motor company, and letters of commendation from Lyndon Johson, Hubert Humphrey and Richard Nixon. In 1980, she was given a used car, her first, by the Volunteers of America. Her success in serving the people of Detroit has come from her absolute faith, which took her through times of great personal difficulty, as well as the trials of keeping her Mission going through very lean years. In 1992, at the age of 76, Mother Waddles was described as an extremely happy person, still vitally engaged in her work. The only thing she has regretted is that the Mission did not have more resources to meet the needs she saw.

From the other end of the socioeconomic spectrum, Cabell Brand, a businessman and entrepreneur, has made a major contribution to the alleviation of poverty in the Roanoke Valley of Virginia, where he founded an organization called Total Action Against Poverty (TAP). From a middle-class background in Salem, Virginia, Cabell Brand built a small, family-owned shoe company into a multi-million dollar corporation. In his early forties, Brand became aware for the first time of the extent of poverty in the nation and began to research the problem. When he realized that money could be made available to the Roanoke Valley to counteract local poverty through the Economic Opportunity Act of 1965 if they made a request and had a valid plan of implementation, he took three months off to study the needs of the area and work out the plan. The result was the formation of TAP. For more than twenty-five years, Brand has been the volunteer president and chairman of the board, often putting in as much as 25 hours a week beyond his own work schedule.

Beginning with the country's first Head Start programs, TAP has grown steadily. There are programs for school dropouts, the elderly, ex-offenders, drug addicts and the homeless, as well as a food bank, a program to bring running water to rural people, home weatherization programs, economic development programs for urban renewal areas and community cultural centers.

Cabell Brand, however, is continually looking to do more. In an interview, he said, "My goal is to take whatever we have learned here in the last twenty-five years dealing with disadvantaged people and see whether there is a way that these lessons can be applied in the rest of the world. Because as I look at it, there's only one problem in the world and that problem is how can 10 billion people live a peaceful, reasonable life on a finite planet."[147]

Vin Quale, a married ex-priest, founded Baltimore's St. Ambrose Housing Aid Center in 1972, and has seen it develop and grow for more than twenty years. While working on racial issues in the inner city of Baltimore as a Jesuit priest, he recognized the need to help poor families take advantage of opportunities to find good, affordable housing. As a result, he studied real estate, becoming an agent so that he could facilitate poor families with buying and selling homes. He also spent time studying other successful housing organizations before he opened the St. Ambrose Center, now considered to be a model housing program in the United States. The Center has staff that will provide counseling, inspect homes, repair homes, negotiate sales, draw up contracts, underwrite mortgages, prevent foreclosures, teach rehab, do rehab, generate housing conversions and make syndication deals. The basic idea of Quale and his organization is that everyone should have a decent place to live.

Quale sees the critical elements in the non-profit world as an informal atmosphere combined with the humor, fun and joy of doing what you are called to do. He also values close relationships with fellow workers who not only share one's dedication but good times as well. A common feeling among those who are serving others is that they do not feel a sense of sacrifice, but of opportunity and privilege.

Many individuals are working quietly throughout the world toward a world peace that would bring a secure future for generations to come. One is a dear friend of mine from Kansas City, Charles Bebb. During World War II, Charlie, a tailgunner, was shot down when his plane was flying over Japan. While spending time in a Japanese prison camp, with plenty of time to think, he decided that there had to be a better way than war to solve the world's problems. Since then, he has spent the better part of his life working for world peace through such organizations as The United Nations Association and World Federalists, who seek to bring world peace through world law.

Detroit, the Roanoke Valley of Virginia, Baltimore and Kansas City are by no means the only places where good people are called to make a difference. Countless communities have such people and organizations. My own community of Aurora, Illinois, a city of more than 100,000 and part of the larger area called Chicagoland, serves as an example of what is being done in other places. Aurora has a full complement of organizations with a national base, counted on by every community: The Salvation Army, Catholic Charities, YMCA and YWCA, The Humane Society, Habitat for Humanity, The Sierra Club, Meals on Wheels, Big Brothers and Sisters, to name just a few.* Aurora also supports local interfaith coalitions that seek to address hunger, homelessness, abuse and youth problems. Many local churches, either individually or with others, sponsor food kitchens and food pantries. An organization in Aurora called Mutual Ground offers services and temporary shelter for women, including their small children, who have been victims of rape and/or of physical and sexual abuse. Besides a temporary place to live, it offers group counseling, mediation, advocacy, some help with education and types of training, and a 24-hour crisis line. There is also the Fox Valley Hospice and the Fox Valley Peace Initiative. For the welfare of animals, there is the Fox Valley Animal Welfare League and Help for Endangered and Lost Pets (HELP).

Another remarkable organization in Aurora is Hesed House. A Hebrew word, "hesed" means compassion and mercy. A not-for-profit coalition of religious ministries serving the very poor, Hesed House originated in 1985 and is now supported by over 125 faith communities in the Fox Valley Area. It is described in their brochure as a "movement of those concerned for the dignity, survival, and reclamation of homeless, hungry, and hopeless people." Their services include an Interfaith Food Pantry and Soup Kitchen. There is a "clothes closet" where over 1600 families and individuals each month are able to select essential items of clothing at no charge.

Advocacy, attempting to influence public policy decisions that affect poor people, is an important part of the Hesed

House program. The stated ultimate goal of all Hesed House ministries is to "eliminate the need for our services because the hungry are fed, the naked are clothed, the homeless have shelter, and people have a chance to hope again." Thousands of volunteers participate in their programs every year, and all consider their work an enriching experience.

Wayside Cross Ministries of Aurora has been providing food, shelter and clothing to those in need for almost 60 years. Unfortunately in recent years, the number of women and children who desperately need aid has been growing. Wayside has responded with a program, co-sponsored by HomeAid Chicago, the philanthropic arm of the Home Builder's Association of Greater Chicago Chrysalis Foundation, and with help from the city of Aurora is a good example of a partnership between public, private and non-profit sectors. The program is titled the Lifespring Ministry for Women and Children.

Although there are many excellent national and international environmental organizations, there is a definite need for smaller groups in communities to monitor the local environment. The Sierra Club does an excellent job of this in many of its local chapters throughout the United States. Most areas of the country also have other environmental organizations as well, such as the Citizens for a Better Environment (CBE), which grew out of the grassroots efforts to increase environmental awareness and stop pollution that began in the late 1960s and early 1970s. Begun in Chicago 25 years ago, CBE has grown to be a regional organization with offices in Illinois, Minnesota and Wisconsin.

From the beginning, CBE's priorities have been to use scientific research, advocacy, public education and citizen empowerment to improve the environmental health of our communities in the midwest. They have been particularly concerned with the impact of environmental degradation on human health. In a new series of initiatives, CBE is drawing attention to dangerous pesticides in the foods people feed their families. In 1996, they released a report that documented 16 pesticides in the nation's most commonly purchased baby foods. They have learned that to achieve real and long-lasting solutions that work for everybody, it is important to work together with the various components of the community-businesses, government and private citizens.

The services of the organizations available in Aurora are duplicated in communities throughout the United States. Yet in spite of the massive work that is being done, the need is greater than can be met thus far. However, as more and more people find their avenue of service, the love and concern that is manifested in good works will serve to lift the consciousness, and thus the well-being, of our country and of the planet.

II. ALL GOD'S CHILDREN: THE THIRD WORLD

In what is often called the "Third World," poverty reaches depths unimaginable to the industrialized societies, even with their widening gaps between rich and poor. Thankfully, many organizations and institutions—international, national, public and private—are dedicated to furthering the alleviation of those desperate conditions.

One of many is Church World Service, an affiliate of the National Council of the Churches of Christ in the USA. For fifty years, Church World Service has "reached out to share help and hope with people in need." They work in partnership with others to meet human needs and foster self-reliance in more than 70 countries, including the United States, through programs of social and economic development, disaster and emergency response and service to refugees.** Through their organizational arm of CROP, they sponsor CROP walks throughout thousands of communities in the United States to raise funds for their many projects. Twenty-five percent of all that is raised in a community stays within that community to address local poverty.

One of the most exciting ideas that has emerged in 1978

to help the poor help themselves is the concept of microbanking. Microbanking consists of making very, very small loans to people too poor to be serviced by regular banks in order for them to start or improve a business. The originator of this concept was Muhammad Yunas, an economics professor in Bangladesh. He realized that what the poor needed was opportunity. When the existing banks refused to participate, Yunas began the project in a very small way on his own. With his first small experiment of empowering poor women with a chance to improve their families' lives, Yunas has shown that offering women small loans used to buy a cow, open a food stall, or launch a fishing boat, is the best way to help families. The payback for these loans was 95%, an extraordinary success rate considering the financial circumstances of the borrowers. His project soon became Bangladesh's Grameen Bank, the largest microbank in the world, which after only a decade had lent over $1.5 billion dollars and provided services to more than 2 million borrowers.

Ten years later, Yunas's inspiration was enhanced by John Hatch's brainchild of village banking. Hatch began the Foundation for International Community Assistance (FINCA). Its function is to support the economic and human development of families trapped in severe poverty. They accomplish this by creating "village banks," peer groups of 25 to 40 members—predominantly women—who receive three critical services: 1) working capital loans to finance self-employment activities; 2) an effective mechanism for promoting family savings; and 3) a community-based system which provides mutual support and encourages self-worth.

The life saving effects of the FINCA program can be illustrated with the story of a destitute Indian woman, whose husband was unemployed and whose children were ill and hungry. She was given a loan of 50 rupees (roughly $1.50). Someone accompanied her to buy herbs and spices, which she was able to sell with a profit of 6 rupees over and above the cost of food to bring home that night. She continued building her business day by day, and the next week, she repaid 51 rupees. A literal life or death situation was resolved with a loan of $1.50.[149]

Since 1984, the FINCA village banking methodology has been used successfully in 14 countries in Latin America, the Caribbean, Africa, and Central Asia, benefiting 86,000 borrowers organized into more than 3,300 village banks. Collectively, these banks are rapidly evolving into a "World Bank for the Poor." Accumulated savings of FINCA village bank members already exceed $4 million.

It rarely happens that technology is brought from the Third World to the rich nations. However, showing the effectiveness of appropriate technology, even for developed countries, microbanking has been brought successfully to the U.S. to address growing poverty here. In recent years it has empowered many American women to free themselves from the welfare cycle.

Although much maligned and criticized due to misinformation as well as lack of information, The United Nations increasingly makes major contributions to the welfare of the planet and its people. Among its many charges, the United Nations regulates the flow of international mail and international air traffic, monitors the import/export of dangerous species, and works to regulate free trade. It has created treaties which protect the oceans; it has decolonized the world; it coordinates international efforts to reduce poverty and disease (through the World Health Organization, it has actually eliminated smallpox); it helps with disaster relief; it promotes a sustainable environment; it helps protect human rights. Although the U.N. has not prevented all wars, it has prevented many and contained others. All this world service was done with a budget for the combined cost of every U.N. program of about $10.4 billion a year, or roughly, one-third the annual budget of New York City. This includes the U.N. peacekeeping initiatives, the World Health Organization,

UNICEF and the High Commissioner for Refugees, as well as the Secretariat. Since its inception, the world's thorniest problems, the ones that individual nations either refuse or are unable to tackle, are continually given to the United Nations, usually with inadequate funding.

The many agencies of the United Nations are continually collecting data from around the world on innumerable subjects of great importance to our continued progress in areas concerning human health and well-being. Robert Muller, a former Under Secretary to the United Nations now serving as president of the Peace University in Costa Rica, is perhaps the foremost advocate of the United Nations. In his book, *Most of All They Taught Me Happiness*, he explained that through his work at the UN he came to believe "that the UN was the greatest school of humanism, universalism and global knowledge that ever existed on earth."[150]

The work toward the elimination of two devastating diseases affecting the Third World, river blindness and iodine deficiency disorders, provides an excellent and heartwarming example of cooperation between the private sector, service organizations and UN agencies. River blindness is transmitted through the bite of a black fly that breeds near fast-flowing rivers and which transmits a parasitic larva, causing intense itching, skin lesions and eventual blindness. Eighteen million people are infected worldwide and in some African communities being blind by age 45 is accepted as inevitable.

Merck & Co., a pharmaceutical company that demonstrates the changing consciousness of enlightened business, developed a drug, Mectizan, which has proven to be a safe and effective remedy for the treatment and control of river blindness. When they realized its potential, Merck & Co. proceeded with its development in spite of the fact that they knew the people it would most help would never be able to pay for it. UNICEF is working with the Non-Government Development Organization Coalition in Nigeria to coordinate a national plan for river blindness control, and has already provided the distribution of 2 million Mectizan tablets, donated by Merck & Co. The U.S. Committee for UNICEF will assist the coalition through fundraising activities in the U.S.

Iodine deficiency impairs normal functioning of the brain and nervous system, causing such abnormalities as goiter, cretinism and a severe form of mental retardation. In Nepal and other parts of the world, it is a serious problem mainly because the people are unaware of the consequences of iodine deficiency. Kiwanis International has pledged to lead a world-wide effort to banish iodine deficiency disorders from the Earth before the end of this century through ensuring salt iodization. They have paired with UNICEF in their hopes to add iodized salt to the diet of every man, woman and child.

•   •   •

In the environmental arena, a recent and exciting program was developed in Sweden by Dr. Karl-Henrik Robert. The Natural Step is a non-profit educational organization. Its purpose "is to develop and share a framework comprised of easily understood, scientifically-based principles that can serve as a compass to guide society toward a just and sustainable future."[151] The premise of the program is that we need to re-examine the negotiable rules of our economic game so they conform to the non-negotiable rules of the biophysical world.

Karl-Henrik Robert points out in the article, "A Compass for Sustainable Growth," that in a democracy, public policy cannot rise above the understanding of the average voter. For that reason, the emphasis of the Natural Step program is on providing the general public with basic knowledge about how the world works. The scientific background of their model is based on the most basic and accepted laws of science. With these laws in mind, the practices of both the public and private sectors can be monitored to see in what ways they violate or sustain the ecosystem. For instance, the content of CO_2 in the atmosphere has increased by 25% due to the use of fossil fuels and deforestation. The proliferation of toxins (over 70,000 chemicals are on the U.S. Toxic Substances Control Act inventory) beyond the capacity of the natural cycles of the biosystem to accept them causes a degradation of our environment and our health. The Natural Step program provides a means by which societies' activities that impact the environment can be monitored and adjusted. "Proceeding back from an absolute framework for sustainability, the economic system can be adjusted with step-by-step investments toward compatibility with the natural system that supports it—i.e., towards sustainability."[152]

The Natural Step model has been successful in Sweden when used by corporations and municipalities. It has proven efficient, not only to demonstrate the need for change, but also as a planning model for concrete economic practice. The successful application of this program in Sweden encouraged its supporters to bring it to the United States. In April of 1996, Natural Step opened its main office in Sausalito, California and has begun training, communications, outreach and administrative operations.

III. "LOVE IS THE ONLY RATIONAL ACT."
Morrie Schwartz

Our emerging paradigm recognizes that the "separate" problems we face in the world are actually interlinked and intercausal. Two problems that are both directly and indirectly linked are racism and violence. Racism poisons the very atmosphere of our social lives, from our smallest communities to our global relationships. It is behind much of the violence that tears the fabric of our societies, from our city streets to wars both within and between nations. Children are most often the victims. Not only do they suffer the consequences of violence, both psychologically and physically—be it within the family or between larger groups—but they also learn how to be violent.

When the temper of violence affects us individually there is often murder; when it affects us in groups, there is often war. A report by UNICEF documents the devastating impact of war on the very young, claiming that warfare is the single largest cause of illness and poverty among the world's children. They report, "During the last decade alone, more than two million children were killed during armed conflicts, more than one million have been orphaned or separated from their parents, 12 million lost their homes, and countless millions remain emotionally scarred."[153]

However, an advanced consciousness is beginning to manifest throughout the world as people invision the reality of oneness. As we realize that humankind is also "interlinked and intercausal," we better understand the impact of our thoughts and actions upon others, both negative and positive. Can we imagine the brightness, the well-being in a world devoid of war? Imagine the resources destroyed in the devastation of war and wasted in the preparation for war diverted to uses that would benefit all of humankind. The world would bloom and our children would flower into the potential that is rightfully theirs. There are many who can imagine such a peaceful world, and they are at work to bring it about. Many organizations, both national and international, are addressing the problems of racism and violence. The several that I mention here are prototypes, ones that I feel get to the very core of the problem—our hearts and minds.

In many communities throughout the United States, citizens are engaged in a program called Study Circles, a diverse community dialogue committed to the elimination of racism. The Topsfield Foundation, Inc., a private, nonpartisan, nonprofit foundation dedicated to advancing deliberative democracy and improving the quality of public life in the United States, has funded The Study Circles Resource Center in Pomfret, CT. The Center carries out its mission by promoting the use of democratic, highly participatory small group discussions known as study circles. The resource center provides materials and guidance for groups throughout the U.S. Their materials are designed to help groups have more productive conversations on some of the most difficult issues our nation faces. Because they believe that dialogue, conducted with openness and respect, with emphasis on both listening and speaking, not only will help to find solutions, but is itself part of the solution, they promote development of a diverse community-wide network of small group discussions on race relations. Mayor David Berger of Lima, Ohio says: "Participants come out of the discussion fundamentally changed. This city will never be the same."[154] In my city of Aurora, Illinois, thousands of people have been through the program, and I believe we all agree with Mayor Berger.

Another program directed to the power of language to both divide and unite was established by Marshall B. Rosenberg, Educational Training Director and Founder of the Center for Nonviolent Communication. For the past 30 years, Dr. Rosenberg and his associates have been providing nonviolent communication training to over 50,000 people in the United States, Europe, Canada, Asia and Africa. According to the Center's information booklet, "Nonviolent communication trains people to use a language that increases good will. It teaches people how to avoid language that creates resentment and lowers self-esteem. It emphasizes compassion as the motivation for our words rather than fear, guilt, blame and shame. It also emphasizes personal responsibility for our choices."

Workshops and intensive training seminars are held each year throughout the United States and in many other countries. For instance, recently in the Chicago area training sessions were given over a three-day period covering various but related topics such as Transforming Violence with Nonviolent Communication, Conflict Resolution in the Workplace, Relationships and Communication, Language of the Heart and From Conflict to Compassion. Through their seminars in Sierra Leone, Hungary, Russia, Israel and Palestine, and Beirut, Lebanon, The Center for Nonviolent Communication has made profound inroads toward nonviolent communication, and thus towards peace. Marshall Rosenberg offers training at the European Peace Studies Program in Austria twice a year. Students from Uganda, Eritrea, Ethiopia, Columbia, and Pakistan have expressed interest in having projects in their countries. According to Rosenberg, their next challenge is to find funds that would allow them to send groups of trainers to countries waiting for their nonviolent communication projects.

One of the most hopeful developments of the last ten or fifteen years is the increased interest in conflict resolution techniques, from the board room to the school room. An organization that has been foremost in cultivating and nurturing this interest is the National Institute for Dispute Resolution (NIDR), founded in 1983. According to their literature, NIDR "envisions a world where people work collaboratively and humanely to find fair and durable solutions to the challenges of conflict which are inevitable in human interaction."[155]

The expressed fourfold mission of NIDR is to 1) deepen humanity's understanding of how constructively to resolve conflict; 2) promote the innovative application of consensus-building processes and conflict resolution skills in the community, state, tribal and national arenas; 3) teach the next generation how to resolve conflicts and avoid violence through collaboration; 4) broaden awareness of, and access to, consensus-building and conflict resolution tools.

They accomplish these goals in several ways, including acting as a clearing house and providing information. NIDR is the largest source of books and other resources in the field of conflict resolution. Through newsletters and a journal, they provide timely and focused information on effective applications of conflict resolutions. They also focus on research, evaluation, and the documentation and dissemination of innovations in the field. NIDR works to publish new books which expand the literature available to the public, as well as teaching and training materials. They also provide networking opportunities for those working in the field and do outreach to communities and institutions.

Much of their focus is on youth; with a network of educational professionals, they seek to bring life skills of non-violent conflict resolution to young people across the nation. Their "goal is to build infrastructures at the local, state and national levels that support the universal teaching—and practice—of non-violent conflict resolutions throughout our schools and neighborhoods." Toward that end they have recently merged with the National Association for Mediation in Education, which has become Conflict Resolution Education Network, now an arm of NIDR. (Although the work of CREN is barely represented in 10% of the total number of U.S. schools, it has been estimated that there are over 8,500 school-based conflict resolution programs located in the nation's 86,000 public schools.)

One of CREN's most successful initiatives is the Peer Mediation Program, in which a cross section of students, usually from 5th to 12th grades, receive 20-30 hours of training to enable them to mediate disputes within their classes or schools. The skills that are learned and practiced within this program are carried over into other conflict situations in both the present and future. From a fifth grader, we hear: "There used to be a lot of fights at school, but not so much anymore because students are learning conflict resolution."[156] A 12th grader who claims being a conflict mediator has changed his view of people, echoes many other students when he says that "being a mediator is a very pleasurable feeling. Knowing that you can help facilitate a minor problem from turning into a major one is [the] ... best feeling in my life."[157]

A recent headline in the Aurora, Illinois *Beacon-News*

illustrates the new concern education has with conflict resolution. It reads, "Teaching Peace Newest Piece of Schoolwork," with the sub-heading: "New skills: Students learning skills that help solve problems, reduce violence." The story commences: "In classroom, lunchrooms and playgrounds of schools, the next generation is learning and practicing peacemaking skills. They're learning to act peaceably instead of violently, learning to use words, not fists or—these days—bullets to resolve problems." Because of the research verifying the effectiveness of these kinds of programs, Illinois legislators have mandated conflict resolution and violence prevention education in schools in a 1993 law. As Ghandi said, "If we are to reach real peace in this world we shall have to begin with the children."

Along with those who serve physical needs and those who teach, those who engage in meditation as a service are also promoting the uplifting of humanity. The light brought in through meditation, consciously directed toward the well-being of all planetary life, illumines the planet and all who are in any way receptive. Most of the "new group of world servers" participate in a variety of these means to serve humankind. "It seems as though," writes Caroline Myss, author of *The Anatomy of the Spirit*, "humanity is 'under orders' to mature spiritually to a level of holistic sight and service, and any number of paths of service to fulfill those orders have opened up to us."[158]

Not only has there been a proliferation of wisdom literature published in the last 40 years or so, both old texts and new, but "wisdom schools" have grown in number and popularity. Both the literature and schools of "higher consciousness" honor the truth in all religious traditions, emphasizing their commonalities rather than differences. They impart the truth of the perennial philosophy, the teachings which have come down through many generations of spiritual traditions.

*This list does not, of course, include all the programs available in the Fox Valley area, but only gives an idea of what is available in most communities.

**It was very encouraging to me that, when working with such organizations as Save the Children and UNICEF, I learned that, indeed, these many organizations do cooperate in their attempts to alleviate hunger and poverty throughout the world.

A human being is a part of the whole called by us Universe, a part limited in time and space. He experiences himself, his thoughts and feelings as something separated from the rest, a kind of optical illusion of his consciousness. The delusion is a kind of prison for us, restricting us to our personal desires and to affection for a few persons nearest to us. Our task must be to free ourselves from this prison by widening our circle of compassion to embrace all living creatures and the whole of nature and its beauty.

Albert Einstein

CHAPTER TEN

FROM CHAOS TO BEAUTY:
HUMANITY'S IMPENDING QUANTUM JUMP

Where there is no vision, the people perish.
Proverbs, 29:18

Our world is rife with visions. The poet Walt Whitman called them "letters from God" left everywhere for us to read. Many have been expressed through teachers, philosophers and mystics throughout the centuries and increasingly today there are visions of new frontiers in human potential, and of the possibilities of a transformed world.

Several principles emerge from the preceding chapters in which we have explored many of these visions. All are in accord with, and in differing ways, actually define the perennial philosophy.

1. There is a Divine Ground, an Ultimate Reality, a Source of all creation, whether it be called, as in Hinduism, Brahman, the unmanifest source of all manifestation; or with David Bohm, the Holomovement, the ground of all manifestation, both expressed and unexpressed; or simply God. This Ultimate Reality is absolute, yet both transcendent and immanent; it is ineffable, yet capable of being realized.

In *Vedanta for the Western World*, Aldous Huxley

summarized the truth he found revealed by the mystical experience which is basic to the perennial philosophy: "... there is a Godhead, Ground, Brahman, Clear Light of the Void, which is the unmanifest principle of all manifestations ... The Ground is at once transcendent and immanent ... it is possible for human beings to love, know and, from virtually to become identical with the Divine Ground ... to achieve this unitive knowledge of the Godhead is the final end and purpose of human existence."[159]

In Taoism it is expressed in the following way.

The Eternal Tao

There is a thing inherent and natural,
Which existed before heaven and earth.
Motionless and fathomless,
It stands alone and never changes;
It pervades everywhere and never becomes exhausted.
It may be regarded as the Mother of the Universe
I do not know its name.
If I am forced to give it a name,
I call it Tao, and I name it as Supreme ...

2. We are more than bones and flesh, or an accident of the universe. Each individual, as well as all Creation, is animated by the Divine Presence. Peter Russell, noted author of *The Global Brain* and *The White Hole in Time*, addresses the question of who we are in the following: "... beyond all our different layers of individuality, beyond all the things we think we are, beyond all the ideas we have, beyond all the different elements of personality and all our hopes and fears, beyond everything, at core, each of us is a droplet of divinity—a manifestation of God."[160] The fact that we are God's creation and animated by his presence and that unity of being underlies the diversity of manifestation is reiterated over and over again within the scriptures of the major religions.

In the last century, the revelations of quantum physics have brought to light a new view of the nature of reality. In *The Spiritual Universe: How Quantum Physics Proves the Existence of the Soul*, physicist Fred Alan Wolf says simply, "We are all connected. Not just human beings, but all sentient life forms." James Jeans, one of the fathers of quantum physics, says that while we may seem to be individuals with separate existences, "in a deeper reality we may all be members of the same body." Paradoxically, the more we become conscious of our connections with the totality of Creation and begin to let go the conditionings and concerns of the separate ego, the more empowered we become as individuals to express the spiritual energy that animates all life.

3. Consciousness is the expression of Being. All Creation is united in having consciousness, but diverse in its depth and expression. With this realization, humanity is also coming to understand that the masculine/feminine natures are a complementary part of a whole—each necessary for the full flowering of our human potential. There is also great diversity in creation, and therefore, diversity in depth of consciousness. Mark Woodhouse, a philosopher and author of *World Views in Transition*, states "God is in all things— right down to the atoms—but not all things are equal in their awareness. That's what makes for differences."

In *The Seat of the Soul*, Gary Zukav equates light with consciousness, and states that the frequency of light that one expresses depends on one's level of consciousness. "You are," he writes, "a dynamic being of light that at each moment informs the [universal] energy that flows through you. You do this with each thought, with each intention."[161] The dynamics of consciousness as a frequency level was forcefully emphasized in chapter six by those who communicated from afterlife dimensions.

Consciousness has only recently become a matter for scientific study, and we are just beginning to plumb its depths. Pierre Teilhard de Chardin, anthropologist, mystic and priest, suggested in *The Phenomenon of Man* that "consciousness ... transcends by far the ridiculously narrow limits within which our eyes can directly perceive it."[162] In the emerging paradigm, the idea pervades that the reality we experience is related to our consciousness and that our experience will change as our consciousness changes. Students of Unity have a simple phrase that expresses this idea. "Thoughts held in the mind, manifest in kind." This wisdom has always been with us. In the Bible it is expressed in Proverbs, 23:7, "For as he [Humankind] thinks in his heart, so is he."

4) Individually and collectively, we are evolving toward a greater awareness and expression of our innate spiritual reality, eventually to become clear channels of Divine consciousness/energy. The idea that we, as humans, even as a planetary system, are evolving is at the core of the perennial philosophy and all the teachings we have found in the previous pages. We know from quantum physics that nothing is static, and from systems and chaos theory that change is truly "the name of the game." Philosophers, mystics, and psychologists see an upward thrust to our destinies. They agree with Tielhard de Chardin that "Life is the rise of consciousness ..."

Implicit in the concept of spiritual evolution is that consciousness not only survives physical life, but continues to grow toward an ultimate state. Aldous Huxley puts forth the premise that whereas "survival is persistence in one of the forms of time, ... immortality is the result of total deliverance," and he suggests that the soul progresses "from mere survival to immortality."[163]

5) We are in control of our destiny, both individually and collectively. We can choose to direct our evolution, or to leave it to a natural, but slower, path. Although individual evolution may proceed apace with the evolution of personal consciousness, the progress of the planet and humanity in general is dependent upon collective consciousness, and there

are no guarantees of sooner or later.

The premise of Teilhard de Chardin's *The Phenomenon of Man* is that evolution has direction and that humanity is moving toward an awakening of latent spiritual powers. Humankind, Teilhard feels, is the "leading edge of evolution," is advancing toward a "super life," and ultimately the Omega Point, the final culmination of our spiritual destiny. However, he does not see this advance as automatic, but the result of our own free will choice. "We are confronted," he writes, "accordingly with two directions and only two: one upwards and the other downwards ..." We must, he feels, learn to "break down the barriers of our egoisms and, by a fundamental recasting of our outlook, raise ourselves up to the habitual and practical vision of universal realities."[164]

Spiritual wisdom teaches that there are two evolutionary paths: the vertical path of awareness and conscious choice, concerned with spiritual growth, the path of the Higher Self; and the horizontal path that is the way of the personality or some would say, ego. This is the path of the lower self, concerned with gratification of physical needs and desires, with consciousness still embedded in the "maya" of materiality. Ultimately both paths lead to the same destination, but the horizontal path is much longer and more difficult, leading through the maze of trial and error, choice and consequence, and the resulting suffering that entails.

The evidence would indicate that a large part of humanity is moving toward the vertical path; also that many, fearing the unknown and the change coming so quickly, are clinging desperately to the familiar lower path. Our world to this point has developed largely through unconscious choice, but now the consciousness of humanity has developed to the extent that we are called to direct our own evolution. Our future lies in the balance with every choice we make.

6. There are spiritual laws that if followed, will make smooth our path and hasten our evolution. The second half of the proverb quoted earlier, "Where there is no vision, the

people perish," is as follows: "but he that keepeth the law, happy is he." Peace Pilgrim, the celebrated "traveler" across the world and on the path of service to God and humankind, tells us that "there are laws governing human conduct which apply as rigidly as the law of gravity. When we disregard these laws in any walk of life, chaos results. Through obedience to these laws, this world of ours will enter a period of peace and richness of life beyond our fondest dreams."[165] These laws are of the most gracious kind and work only to our own happiness and benefit.

All the revealed religions have made the laws and rules of optimal living very explicit within their texts and scriptures. The equivalent of the ten commandments is evident in every religion. It is humbling for those who feel moral exclusivity in their own beliefs to find that the Golden Rule is expressed in every major religious scripture, sometimes in almost identical words. People of all faiths are also told to love God and their neighbors, with "neighbor" defined in the larger sense of all their fellow humans. Indeed, most religions also teach us to treat animals and all creation with respect and love.

Most of us have treated these "laws" as suggestions, but as Peace Pilgrim indicates, when they are broken we must face the results. Karma, the law that every action has its reaction, is not a law of punishment but a law of choice and consequences. It is daunting to realize that we must face the results of not only every word and action, but every thought as well.

•   •   •

"Love always wins."
Morrie Schwartz

If there is any one truth that flows through every chapter of this book, from every teacher, from scientists, from philosophers, from psychologists, from every simple woman or man serving with happiness, it is that love is the most potent force in the universe; that love literally holds the universe together. As Maurice Bucke said, "love is the foundation principle of the world." Teilhard de Chardin has defined love as "an animating energy pulsating through the universe," and "the supreme spiritual energy linking all elements and persons in a universal process of unification." We read in the Bible that "love never fails." Through love we are called to a new tomorrow and a new vision in which "peace 'could' guide the planet and love 'could' steer the stars."

One of the themes of *The Tenth Insight* by James Redfield is that each soul has a life vision—a plan for his or her life which the soul has agreed to before birth; a plan that will allow him or her to employ skills and wisdom gained in previous incarnations, and that will provide opportunity to grow in new directions. At the same time, the life vision of the individual is part of a larger plan for the spiritual evolution of the earth and humanity as a whole. "When we are able," Redfield writes, "to remember what all of humanity is supposed to do, starting right now, from this moment, we can heal the world."[166]

With the more complete "map of the territory" to guide us, which we have received from the perennial philosophy and the revelations of science, perhaps we can not only remember, but pave the way to a better future.

Both birth and death can be painful, but if one searches beyond the death cries of the "old" and the birth pains of the "new," one perceives a higher level of human consciousness beginning to manifest and a New Age of Enlightenment beginning to appear. Martin Luther King, Jr. had the faith that we would prevail, which he expressed in his Nobel Peace Prize acceptance: "I believe that unarmed truth and unconditional love will have the final word in reality."

We are midwives to the future. The choice is ours.

CHAPTER NOTES

CHAPTER 1

1. Walsh, Roger. "The Spirit of Evolution." *Noetic Sciences Review*, Summer 1995.

2. Goswami, Amit. "Quantum Yoga." *The Quest*, March-April 2001: p. 53.

CHAPTER 2

3. Novak, Philip ed. *The World's Wisdom: Sacred Texts of the World's Religions.* San Francisco: Harpers San Francisco, 1994: 13-19.

4. Ibid., 266.

5. Ibid., 217.

6. Ibid., 75.

7. Ballau, Robert O. ed. *World Bible.* New York: The Viking Press, 1954: 152+.

8. Ibid., 31, 106.

9. Novak, 284.

10. Moses, Jeffrey ed. *Oneness: Great Principles Shared by All Religions.* New York: Fawcett Columbine, 1948: 95.

11. Novak, 547.

12. Lin Yutang editor and translater. *The Wisdom of Laotse.* New York: Random House, Modern Library, 1989: 95.

13. Ballau, 556.

14. Lin Yutang, 75.

15. *Baha'u'llah.* Baha'i Publications of Australia, 1991: 11.

16. Ibid., 31.

17. *Gleanings from the Writings of Baha'u'llah.* Trans. Shoghi Effendi. Wilmette, Illinois: Baha'i Publishing Trust, 1976: 104.

18. Ibid., 166

19. Ibid., 286

20. *Baha'u'llah,* 34.

21. *Gleanings,* 96, 215.

CHAPTER 3

22. Boorstein, Seymoor, M.D. ed. *Transpersonal Psychology.* Palo Alto, California: Behavior Books, Inc., 1980: 43.

23. Csikszenthmihalyi, Mihaly. *The Evolving Self: Psychology for the Third* Millennium. New York: Harper-Collins Publishers, 1993: 59.

24. Strauch, Ralph. *The Reality Illusion.* New York: Station Hills Press, 1989: 167.

25. Jung, C. G. *The Undiscovered Self.* Trans. R. F. C. Hull. New York: American Library, Mentor Books, 1958: 14+.

26. Ibid., 100.

27. Ibid., 102-103.

28. Maslow, Abraham H. Toward a Psychology of Being. New York: D. Van Nostrand Company, 1968: 71.

29. Ibid., 79.   *See ** on p 27*

30. Ibid., 80.

31. Ibid., 63.

32. Boorstein, 100.

33. Assagiolio, Roberto, M.D. Psychosynthesis. New York: The Viking Press, 1965: 193.

34. Ibid., 45.

35. de Coppens, Roche. "Psychosynthesis and the Spiritual Tradition." The Quest. Wheaton, Illinois: The Theosophical Society.

36. Ibid.

37. Assagioli, 31.

CHAPTER 4

38. Goswami, Amit, Ph.D. The Self Aware Universe: How Consciousness Creates the Material World. New York: G. P. Putnam's Sons, 1993: 17+.

39. Ibid., 117.

40. Capra, Fritjof. The Turning Point: Science, Society and the Rising Culture. New York: Bantam Books, 1983 80.

41. Davies, Paul. The Mind of God. New York: Simon an Schuster, 1992, 30.

42. Briggs, John and F. David Peat. *Turbulent Mirror: An Illustrated Guide to Chaos Theory and the Science of Wholeness.* New York: Harper and Row Publishers, 1989: 14.

43. Prigogine, Ilya and Isabelle Stenges. *Order Out of Chaos.* New York: Bantam Books, 1984: 12.

44. Briggs and Peat, 110.

45. Ibid., 175.

46. Ibid., 151

47. Talbot, Michael. *Beyond the Quantum.* New York: Macmillan Publishers Company, 1986, 40.

48. Weber, Renee. *Dialogues with Scientists and Sages.* New York: Routledge and Kegan Paul, Inc., 41.   *date*

CHAPTER 5

49. Ghose, Sisirkumar. *Mystics as a Force for Change.* Wheaton, Il.: The Theosophical Publishing House, 1971: 111.

50. Nicholson, Shirley, ed. *The Goddess Re-Awakening.* Wheaton, Illinois: The Theosophical Publishing House, 1989: 130.

51. Ghose, 57.

52. Eisler, Riane. *The Chalice and the Blade.* San Francisco: HarperCollins ,1987: xv+.

53. Stern, Philip Van. *Prehistoric Europe.* New York: W. W. Norton & Company,: 1969: 67.

54. Eisler, 62.

55. Ibid., 63+.

56. Ibid., 31.

57. Cunliffe, Barry, ed. *The Oxford Illustrated Prehistory of Europe*. New York: Oxford University Press, 1994: 43+.

58. Eisler, 59.

59. Nicholson,. 205.

60. Eisler, 139+.

61. Machiavelli, Niccolo. *The Prince*. New York: Dover Publications, Inc., 1992.

62. Ibid., 46.

63. Ibid., 4.

64. Ibid., 14.

65. Ibid., 14.

66. Ibid., 37.

67. Kaye, Howard L. *The Social Meaning of Modern Biology*. New Haven and London: Yale University Press, 1986: 23.

68. Ibid., 23.

69. Ibid., 18, 19.

70. Capra, 44.

71. Ibid., 44 +.

72. Shepherd, Linda Jean, Ph.D. *Lifting the Veil: The Feminine Face of Science*. Boston: Shambhala Publications, Inc., 1993: 1.

73. Ibid., xii.

74. Ibid., 1.

75. Ibid., 20.

76. Ibid., 24.

77. Ibid., 265.

78. Ibid., 174.

79. Ibid., 130.

80. Ibid., 279.

CHAPER 6

81. White, John. *A Practical Guide to Death and Dying.* Wheaton, Il: The Theosophical Publishing House, 1980: 26.

82. Consciousness and Survival: A Symposium. Sponsored by the Institute of Noetic Sciences. An Institute of Noetic Sciences book, 1987: 156.

83. White, 151.

84. *Noetic Sciences Review*, #40, 1996: 44.

85. Doore, Gary, Ph.D., ed. *What Survives.* Los Angeles: Jeremy Tarcher, Inc., 1990: 155.

86. Ibid., 157.

87. Perkins, James A. *Experiencing Reincarnation.* Wheaton, Ill.: The Theosophical Publishing House, 1977: 28.

88. Price, Jan. *The Other Side of Death.* New York: Fawcett Columbine, 1996: 71.

89. Moody, Raymond A., Jr., M.D. *The Light Beyond.* New York: Bantam Books, 1988:8.

90. Price, 47.

91. Ibid., 51.

92. Ring, Kenneth, Ph.d. *Life at Death.* New York: Coward,

McCann & Geoghegan, 1980: 72+.

93. Ritchie, George G., M.D. *Return from Tomorrow.* Grand Rapids, Michigan: Fleming H. Revell, Publisher, 1978: 63.

94. Swedenborg, Emmanuel. *Divine Love and Wisdom.* New York: The Citadel Press, 1965; 150.

95. Atwater, P.M.H. *Coming Back to Life.* New York: Dodd, Meadd, & Company, 1988: 13.

96. Leadbeater, C. W. *The Life After Death.* Wheaton, Il: The Theosophical Publishing House, 1912: 6.

97. Guggenheim, Bill and Judy. *Hello From Heaven.* New York: Bantam Books, 1995: 340.

98. Montgomery, Ruth. *A World Beyond.* New York: Coward, McCann & Geoghegan, New York, 1971: 27.

99. Ring, Kenneth, Ph.D. *Heading Toward Omega: In Search of the Meaning of the Near Death Experience.* New York: William Morrow and Company, Inc., 1984: 83.

100. Ibid., 65, 68.

101. Price, 63.

102. Ibid., 64.

103. Ring, *Heading Toward Omega.* 67, 61, 69, 71.

104. Atwater, 36.

105. Ring, *Heading Toward Omega*, 149.

106. Ring, *Life at Death*, 216.

107. Guggenheim, 15, 32, 35, 85, 154, 168.

108. Ibid., 243.

109. Ibid., 114.

110. Ibid., 343.

111. Redfield, James. *The Tenth Insight*. New York: Warner Books, 1996: 168.

CHAPTER 7

112. Cousins, Norman. *Head First: The Biology of Hope*. New York: E. P. Dutton, 1989: 73.

113. Chopra, Deepak, M.D. *Quantum Healing*. New York: Bantam Books: 69.

114. Ibid., 31.

115. Ibid., 14.

116. Chopra, Deepak, M.D. *Unconditional Life: Mastering the Forces that Shape Personal Reality*. New York: Bantam Books, 1991:165, 166.

117. Siegel, Bernie, M.D. *Peace, Love and Healing*. New York: Harper & Row, Publishers, 1989: 33.

118. Ibid., 253.

119. Cousins, *Head First*, 229.

120. Ibid., 230.

121. Ibid., 37.

122. Chopra, *Quantum Healing*, 193.

123. Robbins, John. *Diet for a New America*. Wallpole, New Hampshire: Stillpoint Publishing, 1987: xvii.

124. Grossman, Richard. *The Other Medicine*. Garden City, New York: Doubleday & Company, Inc., 1985:16.

CHAPTER 8

125. Zohar, Danah and Ian Marshall. *The Quantum Society: Mind, Physics and a New Social Vision.* New York: William Morrow & Company, Inc., 1994: 25.

126. Henderson, Hazel. *Paradigms in Progress: Life Beyond Economics.* Indianapolis, Indiana: Knowledge Systems Inc., 1992:112.

127. Schumacher, E. F. *Small is Beautiful: Economics As If People Mattered.* New York: Perennial Library, Harper & Row, Publishers, 1973: 41.

128. Chappell, Tom. *The Soul of a Business: Managing for Profit and the Common Good.* New York: Bantam Books, 1993:11.

129. Schumacher, 20.

130. World Goodwill Newsletter, 1997, #2, p. 2. New York: World Goodwill.

131. Chappell, 60.

132. Ibid., 95.

133. Covey, Stephen R. *The 7 Habits of Highly Effective People.* New York: Simon & Schuster, 1989: 207.

134. Wheatley, Margaret J. *Leadership and the New Science.* San Francisco: Berrett-Koehler, Publishers, 1992: 27.

135. Ibid., 38.

136. Cantrell, Scott. "An Architect Eyes Energy Conservation." *The Kansas City Star,* 20 August, 1993.

137. *Business Ethics,* May/June, 1996.

138. Wulf, Steve. "The Glow from a Fire," *Time* 8 Jan. 1996.

p 128 Washington Post mess

139. Teal, Thomas. "Not a Fool, Not a Saint." *Fortune* 11 Nov. 1996.

140. *The Wall Street Journal*, 11 June 1991. *3 x copy?*

141. Henderson, 197.

142. Bollier, David. *Aiming Higher: 25 Stories of How Companies Prosper by Combining Sound Management and Social Vision.* New York: The Business Enterprise Trust, 1996: vii, viii.

143. Henderson, 196.

144. *Co-Op American Quarterly*, #41, Spring, 1997.

145. *Noetic Sciences Review #48.* Sausalaito, Ca: Institute of Noetic Sciences, 1999.

CHAPTER 9

146. Clinton, Hilary Rodham. *It Takes a Village.* New York: Simon & Schuster, 1996: 17.

147. Colby, Anne and William Damon. *Some Do Care.* New York: The Free Press, a Division of McMillan, Inc., 1992: 202. *Mother Waddles*

148. Ibid., 231.

149. "Microcredit: A Plan to Help Millions." *International Herald Tribune* 27 September, 1996.

150. Muller, Robert. *Most of All They Taught Me Happiness.* New York: Doubleday & Company, Inc., 1978: 137.

151. Robert, Karl Henrik et al. "The Natural Step News." Winter, 1996. Sausalito, Ca.

152. Ibid.

153. *The Interdependent, UNA/USA,* 1997.

154. "The Busy Citizen's Discussion Guide: Racism and Race Relations," Study Circles Resource Center, Pomfret, Ct.

155. National Institute of Dispute Resolution, Annual Report, 1996.

156. Ibid.

157. Ibid.

158. Myss ,Carolyn, Ph.D. *Anatomy of the Spirit.* New York: Harmony Books, 1996: 277.

159. Ballau, 547.

160. DiCarlo, Russell E. *Towards a New World View.* Erie, Pa.: Epic Publishers, 1996: 370.

161. Zukav, Gary. *The Seat of the Soul.* New York: A Fireside Book, Simon & Schuster, 1996: 106.

162. de Chardin, Teilhard. *The Phenomenon of Man.* New York: Harper & Row, Publishers, 1959: 301.

163. Huxley, Aldous. *The Perennial Philosophy.* New York: Harper & Row, Publishers, 1970: 211.

164. de Chardin, Tielhard. *The Divine Milieu.* New York: Harper & Row, Publishers, 1970: 146.

165. *Peace Pilgrim: Her Life in Her Own Words.* Santa Fe, New Mexico: An Ocean Tree Book, 1994: 30.

166. Redfield, James. *The 10th Insight.* New York: Warner Books, 1996: 168.